Snowflakes All Around

Sarah Lamb

A thank you to my proofreader, Brooke, and all of the lovely women who help ARC read to catch those typos I miss!

Paperback ISBN: 978-1-960418-51-7

CONTENTS

May you always pause in awe at the simple things around you.

CHAPTER 1

Forcing a smile on his face, Kenny waved from the doorway. "See you tomorrow."

His sister, Allison, and her husband called out their goodbyes from inside their cozy house. Kenny closed the door behind him and reached out to still the wreath that was wobbling against the door, feeling some of his tension ease.

It didn't matter they had wanted him there today, and it didn't matter that Kenny usually enjoyed being with his sister and Stuart. There was just the feeling of being a third wheel he couldn't shake.

"Almost wish I hadn't gotten them back together," he muttered, then quickly regretted it the moment the words escaped his lips. That wasn't true, not really. Allison and Stuart were perfect together. Complete opposites, they brought out the best in each other. Well, they did now. It sure hadn't been that way at first.

Besides, if it weren't for them, he wouldn't be here. And this...this paradise, he thought as he looked around him, wasn't something he wanted to be without. He'd never imagined spending his days on a Christmas tree farm, but it had happened, and Kenny wouldn't have traded the peaceful place for anything.

As Kenny stepped off their porch into the chilly late afternoon air, the smell of pine, crisp and exhilarating, struck his nose. Kenny breathed in deeply. He'd never tire of it. It didn't matter the season, this place always carried with it the scent of anticipation.

Living here in one of the cabins on Pressman's Christmas Tree Farm meant he got to be surrounded by all of the future Christmas trees—all of the off-season work—every day.

But Kenny didn't mind at all. Why would he? He enjoyed living here and helping when needed. Besides, Allison and Stuart were family. Everyone who came here was treated that way too.

Just...lately, there was that feeling that didn't seem to leave. Of him being the odd man out. He couldn't mention it to either of them, since he didn't want to risk hurting their feelings. And, right now, Kenny didn't have any future romantic prospects. Wasn't really looking, either, so he really shouldn't be letting himself feel this way.

Overhead, a cloud moved, sending a beam of sunlight onto his cabin, and he grinned at the sight, nature's simple gift lifting his mood. Kenny savored those small, special moments that so many others missed. Like Mother Nature's spotlight on his cabin. And the robin that landed on his roof, singing his song.

The cabins had been built just the year before to provide income for the tree farm throughout the rest of the year—a brilliant idea his sister had come up with to help after a field of trees caught fire—and it had worked. The cabins became an important feature of the place, as did the activities the tree farm hosted, like movie nights and a family fall festival.

Out-of-towners flocked here for a quiet and relaxing small-town weekend. Just last month, they'd had someone from four states away! He couldn't believe it. Things were about to get busier, though.

This was no longer summer, with campfires and s'mores and stargazing or watching movies on the large inflatable screen they had, while swatting gnats and mosquitos.

No, this was just days before winter's opening weekend, when both those who lived nearby and those from far away would descend upon the tree farm to enjoy everything they had to offer while finding their Christmas tree.

And Pressman's Christmas Tree Farm had it all. A trip there was more than just choosing a tree. Guests could munch at one of the food trucks, drink fresh apple cider and steaming hot cocoa, or buy cookies, cakes, pies, and glass jars of preserves from the local women who set them up and sold them. Kenny was hoping for some spiced pear butter. He was running low on last year's stash.

The cold urging him toward the warmth of his heater, he walked the hundred or so yards over to his cabin, the first in the row of eight.

Stuart and Allison had offered it to him rent free in exchange for helping keep an eye on the other cabins when there were guests and assisting with the farm during the busy season.

With as comfortable as these little cabins were, he'd have done that and more in exchange for free rent. They were much nicer than the apartment he used to have, and since he worked remotely, he was able to do his job and be there for the occasional guest needs.

Usually, those were minor. Explaining where something was. Taking over an extra blanket or pillow. Once, he chased out a squirrel that had gotten in. Easy peasy stuff. Someone else cleaned the cabins, so he didn't have to do much with that aspect. But with him living right there, and having access to the storage areas, it was much quicker for him to help a guest, and happy guests meant good reviews and full bookings.

As for helping around the tree farm, tree-buying season was when he was busiest, helping do everything from setting out tables to cleaning up or driving the tractor out to fields with loads of guests on the back trailer, ready to saw down their choice of trees. It was always fun to watch them squint and frown, seeking the perfect pine among thousands.

Kenny stepped onto his porch and breathed in deeply once more before he unlocked his door. "I'm home," he sang out to Goldie, the fish he'd bought when he first moved in. He knew he could have another pet, but he was worried about it being lonely when he wasn't home, or running away and getting hurt with some of the equipment the tree farm had, like a cat or dog might.

Goldie made him happy. She swam soothingly around her tank when she wasn't hiding in the little castle he'd bought her. She also was a champion bubble blower. Kenny was sure she must have won awards for that, in her old neighborhood.

"Let's see, guest list," Kenny mumbled, pulling out the papers his sister had given him and attaching them to the clipboard on his wall. "Who might need a little help this week, Goldie?" Kenny ran his finger over the dates and names. Looked like five guests this week. Then, full cabins the week after. As was to be expected.

During the holidays, and the weeks leading up to them, the cabins were almost always booked. They stayed that way during summer too. Especially now that word had gotten around about how nice and also reasonably priced they were.

Of the eight cabins, five had two bedrooms, with a living space and small kitchen and bathroom. That's the type he lived in. The last three were for larger groups, like families, and had three bedrooms. All of them had a front porch with two rocking chairs, and a patio out back with benches and a small firepit.

Kenny wandered over to the kitchen and made himself a Sunbutter sandwich with strawberry jelly and a few handfuls of barbeque chips on the side. As he passed by his living room window, he saw a small blue car pulling up to the cabin next door.

He glanced at his list of guests. That must be Merry Douglas. She was the only one scheduled to arrive today.

Merry. Now there was a name perfect for this time of year. Was she also a cheerful sort of person?

He tried to answer his question by watching as she got out of the car, but her back was to him. The woman walked to the rear of her car and raised the trunk, presumably getting her luggage.

"What's wrong with me?" Kenny asked. He didn't know why he was still staring at her. He should walk away. Or even go outside and see if she needed help. But he felt frozen to the spot.

It seemed like forever before the car's trunk closed and he got his first look at Merry. Blonde hair in a thick braid over her shoulder, a warm jacket, fuzzy hat, boots, and jeans. Pretty normal attire for this time of year.

But what wasn't normal were the tears streaking down her face.

Kenny's stomach jolted. He wasn't sure why. He hadn't ever felt this way before after seeing someone. His mouth suddenly felt dry, and he swallowed hard.

The woman lugged her suitcase and a large bag to the front of her cabin and went inside without even looking around. But Kenny couldn't stop staring at her closed door. Suddenly, he realized what he was doing, and stepped away from the window.

"She'll think I'm a creep, Goldie," he said. "Staring like that."

Goldie shimmied her fins.

"Glad you don't," he told his fish, dropping a few flakes of food in her bowl. "I don't know what came over me. That was...weird."

Kenny took his lunch over to the couch and flicked on the TV, planning to settle in with an action movie. However, the only things playing were Christmas movies and game shows.

"Not a problem," he said between bites. "Tis the season for happenings in the snow."

Kenny settled further into his seat, trying to take his mind off the woman he'd just seen. It was hard, though. Kenny wanted to rush over and see if he could help her or make her feel better. But last time he'd tried something like that, he'd gotten punched in the nose. Twice. Once by the woman who thought he was a masher, and then again by her boyfriend, who thought he was moving in on his girl he'd just had a fight with.

Still, he supposed it had worked out. The couple had gotten back together, and his nose hadn't broken. He reached up and rubbed at it. That was something, he guessed. But it was also the thing that reminded him not to stick his nose into the business of others.

Still...looking after others had always been something he did. Working here had given him more opportunities to do that, and he loved it. There was nothing better than that feeling of knowing you made a difference in someone's life, even if it was just in a small way.

He was about halfway into a movie where a big city girl fell in love with the small-town guy who healed her heartache when it came to him. While he wasn't necessarily looking for love like the characters were in the movie, maybe this was his opportunity to work a Christmas miracle himself.

Merry hadn't seemed very...well, merry. Could he change that? Find out what was wrong and bring a smile to her face? Goldie started swishing frantically, as though she thought it were a wonderful idea, and Kenny nodded. "Yes. I think I can, Goldie."

Chapter 2

"Turn left in a quarter mile."

"Got it," Merry Douglas said to her car's GPS. She slowed down and clicked her signal on.

"Make a U-turn," the GPS said.

"Umm, wait. I haven't turned left yet," Merry said.

"Recalculating route," the monotone GPS replied.

"What are—"

"Turn right in one mile."

"But—"

"Make a U-turn."

"But I'm—"

"Recalculating. Recalculating. Recalculat—"

"I'll recalculate you," Merry snarled, reaching over and smacking at the navigation unit. "I hate this stupid thing. Why can't you ever work? I wish my phone wasn't dead."

"Turn left."

Merry sighed deeply. "Fine. I'll turn left." As she took the left, a small town came into view.

"Oh, thank goodness. This looks promising. Maybe I can ask someone where I am."

Just then, her car gave a weird shiver, and made a loud thunking sound.

"Oh no!" Merry cried, and smacked the steering wheel. "A flat? What else will go wrong?"

Luckily, there was a gas station ahead. Maybe someone could help. She slowed and pulled into the station, taking one of the few parking spaces available. The station was tiny, but it was better than being stranded in the middle of nowhere. As she climbed out to look at her tires, she winced. Yep. It was a flat. There was no missing the huge screw in her front tire.

Merry bit her lip and glanced around. From here, it was impossible to see if there was a repair shop. Maybe someone would know inside. She locked her car and walked into the small convenience store attached to the two-pump gas station.

"Welcome," a woman said cheerfully, setting down the historical romance novel she was reading. Merry peeked at the title. *A Sleigh Ride for Charlotte.*

"Thanks," Merry said. "Hey, I've got a flat. Is there anyone in town who can help me? I'm not from around here. I had come to stay at Pressman's Cabins, but there's no way I can make it on that tire."

"Ooooh those are nice cabins, I hear," the woman said. Then she shook her head. "We don't have a tire place around here, but there is a mobile mechanic. Want me to call him?"

"Can you?" Merry asked. "I'd really be grateful. My phone is out of charge and the cable to charge it broke when I went to plug it in."

"Sounds like you're not having much luck today," the woman said sympathetically.

"Nope," Merry said with a small laugh. It was either that or cry, right? And right now, she was really feeling the urge for the latter.

"I'll call now."

The woman picked up the phone, and Merry wandered through the small store, grabbing a soda, a pack of gum, some chips, and a cup of fresh-ish looking grapes. There was even a cable for her phone, which she pounced on. She returned to the counter and set the items down, then fished through her purse for her credit card.

"Someone will be here in a jiffy," the woman said, ringing up her items and bagging them.

"Thanks," Merry said. "I appreciate it."

She walked back out to her car, her eyes on the deflated tire. Merry opened her door and sat, sighing. "This too shall pass," she mumbled—her grandmother's favorite phrase whenever anything happened.

At least she had help on the way, and she could get her phone charged. Merry connected her phone and waited while it powered back on. Several emails popped up, but the one from Tammy's Travels caught her eye. She tapped on it, and her stomach sank as she read the email. It was short and to the point.

Merry, I'm not happy with these ads. I want a playful, imaginative aspect. Something fresh, new. Not just people lounging around with smiles. When people see the ad, I want them to think this is it! I can go here, rejuvenate, unplug, experience the magic of nature. This is the third time you've redone these for the forest getaway. Send me something new next week, but if I don't like it, I'm sorry. I'll need to find someone else. It's nothing personal, just business.

Merry sucked in a breath and closed her eyes. The words echoed in her head. *Find someone else.*

She didn't want that. This was her biggest client. They'd been together for a little over two years and until now, she thought they'd been happy with her work. But this whole playful, imaginative, rejuvenated thing. What did that even mean? How in the world could you make a forest getaway imaginative and playful?

Merry closed out of her email and rested her head on the seat back. There would be time to worry about that later. Right now, she couldn't do anything until her tire was fixed.

The bag of chips, soda, and most of the grapes later, a red truck pulled up and an older man climbed out, eyeing her car. "You got a flat. Did you know that?"

"I did," Merry said. "The woman inside was going to call someone to help repair it."

"That would be me," the man said. "Won't take long."

Merry nodded, and waited on the curb in front of the shop, her fuzzy hat on her head and her jacket zipped as high as it would go. It wasn't the coldest here, but it sure wasn't warm, by any stretch of the imagination.

The old man pulled off her damaged tire, and took it to the back of his truck. Merry pulled up the map app on her partially charged phone and tried to study the area. It was useless. She had almost no signal. She'd blame that being the reason her GPS was acting so wonky, but she had to be honest. When had the silly thing ever worked properly?

She hoped she was close to the cabins. All she wanted right now was to find them, make herself comfortable, and then cry.

She glanced over at the man who was humming a song she couldn't place. "About done," he assured her, and sure enough, not much later he was putting the tire back on her car.

"Thank you," Merry said. "How much do I owe you? I hope you take credit cards?"

"Sure do," he said, taking her offered card and typing some things into his phone. "Usually I charge fifty, but Meggie in there told me you were having a rough day. I'll knock it down to forty."

"I appreciate it," Merry said.

"Think nothing of it." When he returned the card to her, he said, "Good as new. Watch out for where you drive, though."

"I'll try," she said, climbing back into her car. "Thank you again for the discount. That was really nice of you."

"My pleasure," he said, starting to walk away.

Merry stuck her head out the window. "Wait just a second! I'm looking for Pressman's Cabins. Do you know where they are?"

"About two miles down the road, follow the signs for the Christmas tree farm," the man told her. "Cabins are on his property."

His truck roared to life, and he drove away before Merry could pick her jaw up from the ground. The cabins were on the property of a Christmas tree farm? That meant loads of people bustling around, likely cheerful music and activities and all those other things she wasn't wanting to experience right now.

She'd chosen a cabin to get away. Hide. Merry wanted quiet. Time to wallow in her misery. Not to be surrounded by crowds of noisy people. How had she not noticed this when she booked the cabin? What next?

Not that she wanted to invite anything more. It was bad enough that her marketing business, which she'd poured her heart and soul into for years, was crumbling down around her.

Because of the economy, some of her clients had put their needs on hold. Others scaled back. Bills were piling up, her laptop she needed for work was on the fritz, and Merry was concerned she wouldn't be able to make it financially until the end of January if she lost Tammy's Travels. The last few months had been really difficult.

She'd been hustling. Offering new packages. Even going door to door, swallowing down her pride. Times were tight, though. No one was interested.

Her business was a failure. She was a failure. Heck, right now even her usually snug little apartment was failing her, with burst pipes and no heat. And then, the cabin she'd rented at a near steal, with the desperate idea that she just needed a few days to reset while her apartment underwent repairs, turned out to be on a Christmas tree farm. Where there would be festivities and happiness. She just wasn't in the mood for that. And now, she'd have to work while trying to get some peace and quiet.

But Merry knew she shouldn't be surprised. This was just another thing she'd failed at. Picking a weekend getaway. What was wrong with her? Maybe her grandmother was right when she said dreams were pointless. Owning her own business had been a dream come true, but now it was slipping through her fingers.

Work had always been something solid to hold on to. Something to focus on. It was real. But maybe even that had been an illusion.

Merry drove in the direction the man had indicated and was relieved to see numerous signs pointing her toward the tree farm. She finally clicked the turn signal on and pulled onto a long gravel driveway. This, at least, had gone easily. Her tires crunched as she followed one more sign, pointing toward the cabins that she could now see at a distance.

This morning, she'd gotten an email saying the key would be under the mat of Cabin #2, so she hoped it was. It had been a rough day, and she just wanted to relax, not track down whoever ran the place.

Luckily, the cabins were each marked well, and there were only two other cars. Maybe it would be quiet and this wouldn't turn out to be too bad after all.

But then again, luck sure hadn't been on her side as of late. Maybe this picturesque landscape would actually be the setting of her next problem.

When she climbed out and smashed her fingers while pulling her suitcase from the back of her car, Merry let her tears finally fall. Yep. Just as she'd thought. Nothing was going well. She might as well get ready for a few more days of it.

CHAPTER 3

Kenny paced back and forth. He started toward his front door but stopped just as his hand reached the knob. He repeated the entire process several times, each instance causing him to grow more and more aggravated with himself. What was wrong with him? This was part of his job.

All he needed to do was walk over, introduce himself, hand her a schedule of events, and see if she needed anything. He'd done this a hundred times. More, actually. So why did this time feel so different?

Gulping in a deep breath, Kenny pulled open the door. Then he closed it, and leaned over, hands on knees. He'd never felt so nervous in his life. He almost felt like throwing up. It was as bad as when he was in third grade and played Snowman Number Four in the school holiday play. Kenny closed his eyes and willed himself to straighten.

"Got to do it," he said to Goldie, who swished her tail at him encouragingly.

This might have been the one time he wished he had a small dog to take on a walk. What woman could resist a cute fuzzball? He sure couldn't take Goldie out. That would be strange.

Kenny sighed and opened the door, his legs carrying him over to Cabin #2 before he could quite realize it. He knocked on the door and stepped back slightly. As he waited, he tried breathing in slowly to calm his racing heart.

The door started to open, and Kenny snapped his attention to it. The woman who was peeking through. "Hello?"

"Hi! I'm Kenny," he said. "I work here at Pressman's Cabins."

"Oh. I see." She relaxed slightly and opened the door a little wider. "How can I help you?"

"I actually wanted to see if there was anything you needed. Is the cabin to your liking?" he asked, finding some comfort in the familiar question he asked new cabin guests.

"It's great. Thank you," she said.

"We've got a bunch of events coming up," Kenny told her, offering her the paper in his hand. "I hope to see you at a few."

"Oh, thanks, but you can keep it," the woman told him. "I don't plan to leave my cabin."

His brow furrowed. "You don't? But there's so much to do right now. You came at our busiest time of year." He pointed to the paper. "There's more than just getting a tree. Food trucks and a movie under the stars, wreath making, candy making—"

"I'm good. Thanks." The woman started to shut her door.

"I don't mean to be rude," Kenny said. "A no is a no. I was just surprised."

She stopped, and sighed. "I know. I appreciate it. It's just that it's been a rough day. Rough month too. I'm just not in the mood to celebrate or have fun or anything like that. I hope you understand. I just came here for quiet and to work."

He nodded slowly. "Sure. I understand. But, if you need anything, let me know, okay? I'm next door, Cabin #1. And my name is Kenny, in case you forgot."

"Thanks," the woman said. She hesitated, then said, "I'm Merry."

"Good to meet you, Merry," Kenny said. He backed away slowly, putting the schedule into his jacket pocket.

That had been weird. Really weird. She didn't even just take the paper to shut him up. Maybe that's what felt strange to him. Who wouldn't at least grab it to be polite? He'd done that himself, and then just thrown it away later.

Not that she'd been rude. Kenny hadn't missed the sadness in her eyes or the catch in her throat when she'd said it had been a rough day. That was likely why she'd been crying as she walked to the cabin. He wondered what could have been so terrible that she was so upset.

He hesitated, then posted the schedule on the community board. There. If she wanted to see, she still could. If she didn't, then at least he'd tried. He was going to have to put one there anyway.

Kenny jammed his hands into his coat pockets, and started across one of the tree fields. He could see a figure in a bright red jacket, holding a yardstick.

"What's up, sis?" he asked as he got closer.

She rolled her eyes. "Stuart is making me measure the trees again to find the four-footers. He thinks I might have done it wrong."

"Maybe you did?" he asked, watching her. "Not like either of us knows too much about his measuring method. Yet."

She sighed. "Yeah. I'm sure you're right. I'll have to have him show me again. I've forgotten." She studied her brother, and Kenny tried not to squirm. She was giving him the same look their mom did when she was on to him. "What are you up to?"

"Nothing, just you know, being neighborly," he said. "Said hello to Cabin #2. Offered the schedule."

He dug the tip of his sneaker into the mulch by the tree, watching as a piece skittered away.

"Hey."

At his sister's soft voice, Kenny looked up. "Yeah?"

"You aren't usually so serious or quiet unless something's wrong. I mean, you haven't made fun of me once since you came out here. That makes me worry something's going on."

"You've got Stuart now to pick on you," Kenny said with a wink. "I thought you'd appreciate the break from me."

His sister laughed and shook her head. "You know what I mean. Something's on your mind. Want to tell me?"

Did he? Kenny wasn't sure. And it was because he didn't know what was wrong. If anything was. There was just this weird...

"Feeling," he blurted.

"What?"

"There's just this weird feeling I've got. When I talked to the woman in Cabin #2. Maybe even before I went there."

"Oh?" Allison furrowed her brows, giving him her full attention. "Should we be concerned?"

"Not like she's a serial killer or something," he assured her. "Her name is Merry, and she's just...real sad." Kenny frowned, and let his gaze fall on the tree in front of them. He reached out, letting the prickly pine jab his fingers, bring him back to the present. "She's just so sad, Allison. And for some reason, it gets to me."

His sister nodded. "That's because you're a good person." She reached over and squeezed his arm. "You've always been able to pick up on things others can't. But you shouldn't let yourself feel responsible for fixing things for everyone. She's a stranger. If she needs something, she'll tell you."

"Yeah, I guess you're right. It's just this time is different. Feels different. Like, I can't seem to just say, 'Gee, that's too bad,' and keep going. I don't think this is just me wanting to help to be nice. I can't explain it, but I want to do something to make her feel better."

"Just be you. It will come if it's meant to. You'll see." Allison squeezed his arm.

"I don't know," Kenny said doubtfully. "Does anything ever happen that way?"

She laughed. "It will. Trust me. Hey, didn't you make things work out for me?"

"Well, that was different," Kenny said. "You and Stuart were both—"

"Ahhh, we don't need to remember that," Allison said, waving her hand around. "What matters is that in the end, you made me happy, Stuart happy, and the whole town happy, when we managed to save Christmas for a whole lot of people."

"Yeah. Yeah, we did, didn't we?" A slow grin formed on Kenny's face.

"Maybe this woman—did you say her name was Merry?—maybe she just needs a little dose of Christmas magic too." Allison swept her arms wide. "There's a ton of it here, as I've learned. Give her a chance to find it."

"There sure is. We are pretty good at manufacturing it. And wait...give her a chance to find it? That's a good idea." Kenny nodded slowly to himself. Maybe he could be the one to help her find it. Make her smile. Make things not feel so bad. Kenny liked that idea. It felt good. Felt right.

"I've helped you, now you help me," Allison said. "Hold this yardstick and measure. Between the two of us, we've got to figure it out."

Kenny smirked, but did as she said. Older sisters were bossy, and there was no getting away from it. But as she held the stick this height and that, he couldn't help but hope he saw Merry again soon. He wanted to talk to her, since that would be the best way to figure out what kind of Christmas magic she needed, so he could provide it.

CHAPTER 4

Merry hadn't missed the way Kenny's expression had been one of surprise when she told him she didn't want the activity schedule. She also didn't miss how his shoulders had slumped a little as he'd walked away.

She watched as he tacked the paper to a small community board, wondering why it mattered to her that he'd seemed almost disappointed she hadn't taken it. He was a stranger. She'd never see him again.

But, he was in the cabin next door. So she might. That could make things...awkward.

"If I see him again, I'll apologize," she promised herself, watching Kenny walk away.

Then, she sighed, and went over to the couch, where she threw herself down on it and picked up her laptop. Merry browsed ads for travel agencies, hoping to get some marketing inspiration. But everything she saw was just what she'd been doing. Merry had prided herself on being on brand.

But it seemed that wasn't what Tammy wanted anymore. What she did want wasn't something Merry could find examples of. Frustration filled her. She had to figure this out if she wanted any chance at all to save her business. She'd worked too hard to just give up.

But what if I can't?

The thought jolted her, and Merry frowned. Hard work always paid off. She just needed to try harder.

When her stomach gurgled, Merry glanced at the time and realized it had been ages since she'd eaten, and it was almost dinner time. She'd come prepared with a few food items in her suitcase, but as she poked through, nothing she'd brought sounded good.

"Food trucks," Merry said. "He mentioned food trucks, didn't he?"

She tried to peek from the window, but she wasn't able to see much from her angle. Except for the board where Kenny had tacked up the notice.

Merry grabbed her jacket and hat and went to look at it. Wouldn't hurt just to look. And, if there was a truck, reward herself after a long day with something she didn't have to cook. She'd splurge just this once. Maybe even see Kenny and apologize. Once that was done, maybe she could concentrate.

The wind had died down, making the air feel crisp, not bitter. Merry breathed in deeply. The area smelled so clean. It was nice. She was glad she'd gotten away, even if it was just delaying her facing the inevitable. Maybe the fresh air would clear away her stagnant thoughts, though. She was sure hoping.

Merry wandered over to the schedule Kenny had posted and browsed it. There were food trucks listed, and for the entire weekend. She felt in her coat pocket. Yep. She had some cash. Time for dinner.

The faint sound of music played in the air, and Merry followed it. The sun was just starting to set. She planned to grab a bite and head back to her cabin to see what was on TV. Maybe there was a cheesy movie to help her get some advertising ideas. She just wished she could stop worrying for a few moments so that she could relax enough for ideas to come.

Up ahead, she could see white Christmas lights strung across a large set of poles stuck in the ground. There were dozens of people walking around, a huge Christmas tree, and at a short distance past that, the food trucks. Children ran near a huge inflatable movie screen, presumably waiting for it to get a little darker. Everyone seemed relaxed. Maybe some of that would come her way.

Merry stood a few paces away and perused her choices: a BBQ truck, a taco truck, and a mac and cheese truck. There was also a dessert truck and one selling hot drinks.

"Tough choice, isn't it?" a voice asked.

Merry turned and saw Kenny. He was focused on the food trucks. "I hate the nights that Nina's Tacos and Paul's Mac n Cheese are both here. I can never choose."

She would have laughed at the puppy dog expression on his face and in his voice if she hadn't felt the same.

"Will they both be here tomorrow?" she asked.

"Yep," Kenny said. "Same old problem."

"Nah. One tonight," Merry said, walking toward the mac and cheese, "and one tomorrow."

Kenny stared at her, surprise on his face. She did laugh then, as he asked, "Why didn't I ever think of that?" He started to follow her, then paused. "You won't think I'm creepy if I get the mac too, will you? I just really want it."

"I won't," she promised.

It was weird. They'd hardly interacted, but...Merry was feeling lighter. Maybe it was the festive mood here. She hadn't wanted to be, but she was swept up, just a little.

As she waited for her food, Merry let her eyes roam around. "It's really pretty here," she said. "The lights are a good touch, and everyone seems in a good mood."

Kenny nodded. "Stuart and Allison work hard to make sure everyone enjoys themselves."

"Are they the owners?" Merry asked.

"Yep. Stuart Pressman," Kenny said, pointing to a man near the large Christmas tree, "and that's Allison. In the red jacket. She's my older sister. They got married a few months ago."

"Oh! So do you work here with them year round?" Merry asked, taking the container of her mac and the plastic fork.

"Allison still works during the day for the local insurance company. I do too, in IT," Kenny told her, grabbing his dinner too. "But I get to work remotely, so I'm here to help as they need me. That includes checking on guests and making sure they are okay. In trade, I get free rent."

"Nice," Merry said. She considered taking her food back to her cabin, but it was actually really pleasant being out here. Maybe it wouldn't hurt to stay just while she ate.

She walked to one of the picnic tables and sat. Kenny sat across from her. Steam wafted from up her mac and cheese, and she took a bite. "Mmm! This four cheese is so good."

"I love the bacon one," Kenny told her. "Paul's the best at this."

Merry ate a few more bites, watching as everyone seemed to cluster around the Christmas tree. Children and adults tied pieces of paper onto the tree. "What are they doing?" she asked.

Kenny looked over. "Oh! That's the wishing tree. You grab a piece a paper ornament, we've got 'em in all shapes, and you write a wish on there. Then you hang it up."

"What are the wishes for?" Merry asked.

"Just to put out there into the universe," Kenny said. "Though, sometimes people wander past and recognize someone's handwriting, or the writer puts a name on there, and a wish gets fulfilled. It's just a little thing right now; this is only the second year for it. Maybe it will become a tradition." He shrugged and took another bite.

Merry watched as more people came up to the tree. She assumed they were from town. There were more people than cabins. Some laughed as they hung their wish. Others looked thoughtful or even sad.

"Have you hung one up?" she asked. Then she quickly said, "That was rude of me. I'm sorry. And I'm also sorry for earlier. I wasn't trying to be ungrateful about the schedule. I was just tired. It's been a rough day."

"So you said," Kenny told her, his warm eyes meeting hers. "If I can help in any way, let me know."

Merry just nodded, not wanting to explain more.

"But it's not rude or nosy or whatever. I did put a wish on the tree, just before I went to the food truck," he told her.

She wondered what it was. Was there something Kenny wanted? If she were to write a wish—not that she'd do anything so silly—what would it be?

He winked at her. "I'll tell you mine. I don't mind," he said.

"What was it?" she asked, now curious.

A serious look came over his face. "I just want to make someone smile," he told her. "That's all."

Merry blinked a few times. "That seems like a strange wish. Make someone smile? Someone in particular?"

"Yeah," Kenny said quietly. "I'm not sure what's going on, but I think they really need some Christmas magic right now."

A little tug pulled on Merry, and she tried to ignore it, instead taking the last bite of her dinner.

"So, how do you like your cabin?" Kenny asked.

She was glad for the change of topic.

"I love it," Merry said. "It's adorable and cozy. There's a great view of the farm too."

"Yeah, it's way bigger than you'd think," Kenny said.

"Oh yeah? Am I allowed to walk around and see for myself?" she asked.

"Sure! And—"

"Kenny! Can you start the movie?" a woman called.

"Oops! Got to go! Allison can't ever get the DVD system going," Kenny said, jumping up. "See you later."

"Bye," Merry said, watching as he jogged over to his sister, standing in front of a complicated looking audio visual setup. She didn't blame Kenny's sister. She probably would have trouble too. The guy Kenny called Stuart was there too, pushing at buttons until Kenny shooed him away, and started the DVD with a few taps.

The movie *Elf* started, and everyone quieted, settling down in chairs. Firepits snapped and popped, giving warmth to those who wanted to sit or stand near them.

Merry stood and threw her trash away, intending to head back to her cabin. While she liked the movie, she needed to try and work. Time was limited, and now that she was alone again, all she could think about was her deadline.

She knew if she relaxed, ideas might flow to her easier, but she couldn't. This wasn't just about keeping her client. It was about financial security. Something she hadn't grown up with, and really longed for.

As she passed by the table nearest the large Christmas tree, she saw the paper cutouts and pens. There were stars and bells, trees, and gingerbread men to write on.

Without quite knowing why, Merry picked up a pen, and scrawled her wish on a red star. Then, she hung it on a tree, right next to one she knew must be Kenny's. It read, *I just want to make her smile.*

There was a silly little tightness in her chest, a surge of jealousy, of emptiness. Who did he want to make smile? A woman he liked? Whoever she was, she sure was lucky. Merry wished for a little of that. Not only was her life falling apart, but she didn't have anyone to share it with.

CHAPTER 5

Kenny watched as Merry wrote a wish, and then placed it next to his. Had she known that was his wish? Nah, couldn't have. He'd written it before he'd even seen her.

He stepped back and watched the movie for a moment, made a small adjustment to the sound, then wandered over toward the tree. He wanted to see what she had written.

Glancing around to be sure no one saw, he looked for the spot he'd seen her place her wish. There it was, on a red star. Kenny leaned close to better read it in the night lit only by twinkling stars and tiny white Christmas lights.

I wish I could save my business and maybe find a little happiness.

He stepped back and frowned. Save her business? Maybe that's why she seemed so unhappy. That was a tough thing to have happen, especially at this time of year. Not that there was ever a good time of year to lose a business or a job, but around the holidays, when people were happy and smiling and in a good mood...Kenny could see how that would make her feel so much worse.

He studied her wish while his mind worked furiously. If he could figure out a way to help her wish come true, then his would as well. He could make her smile.

The second part of her wish made him feel just as pained as the first did. She wanted to find a little happiness somewhere.

His earlier conversation with his sister trickled through his mind. *A dose of Christmas magic.* There was happiness and beauty all around in so many small things and moments. Sometimes people just needed to be shown it, when they were at that point where everything looked bleak.

That was also something he could do. That was something he *would* do. Kenny hurried over to his sister. "Hey, you need me anymore tonight?"

"Are you feeling okay?" Allison asked. She put a hand to his forehead. "Is your throat hurting?"

She was so much like their mom, Kenny had to laugh. "I'm fine, sis. I just need to get a little work done."

"Oh. Of course," Allison said, and rolled her eyes. "Sorry. I forgot. The IT system upgrades."

"Yep. I want to get them finished so I can help around here the next few days to get the rest of the decorating done."

"I appreciate it," his sister told him. "Go, I got this. I just unplug it all, right?"

"Yeah. But push the red power button before you do," Kenny said.

"Right. I can do that."

"Come get me if you need help," Kenny told her.

"I'm fine, fine!" Allison said, and walked away backward, giving him a double thumbs up.

He tried not to wince. Hopefully, the audio-visual setup would survive her. And if it didn't, all was well. He'd convinced Stuart to get the extended warranty.

Kenny headed back to his house and turned the heat up. A few minutes later, he was sitting at the table, laptop in front of him, a soda nearby, and a bowl of popcorn still steaming. He worked for about an hour, but his mind kept wandering back to Merry.

"Got to finish this first," he told himself.

From the corner of his eye, he saw Goldie shimmy, obviously in agreement.

Two hours later, Kenny checked that all the systems were working after the new software install, and then yawned and pushed away from his laptop. He reached for the soda, but it was empty. When had that happened?

It was getting late, but Kenny had one more thing to do before he could sleep. He rummaged around in the closet and found the picnic basket that he'd won last year at the insurance company's party. He hadn't used it yet, but now was the perfect time. Kenny set it on the counter. In the morning, he'd put his plan into motion.

Making Merry smile.

But when the sun was up and he found himself standing on her porch knocking, the basket in one hand, Kenny worried he'd made a bad decision.

"A picnic?" Merry asked. "It's like...thirty degrees out."

"Thirty-four," Kenny said, showing her his weather app. "Trust me. I've got a plan."

Merry raised an eyebrow. "Is this how you treat all the guests? Personalized picnics and tours?"

"No. You're special," he said, before he realized what he'd just said. Kenny was pretty sure his cheeks were as red as his scarf. "I mean—"

"Let me get my jacket." Merry shut the door, and Kenny sat in one of the porch chairs, trying not to panic.

What did she think of him? That he was weird? He sure sounded weird. Ugh. She'd think he was a creep for sure. Chances were good, she was calling 911 right now. Wouldn't come out. Allison and Stuart would be so mad at him. He might even lose his IT job, if they thought he was stalking people! When had he become such a nervous wreck? He'd never felt this way around anyone before. But Merry was different, and—

The door creaked open. "I'm ready," Merry said, coming outside. "I've got a package of cookies to add. But the sky looks strange. Think we'll get snow?"

"It's a little hard to say," Kenny told her, leading the way. He pointed in the distance. "That mountain ridge there, and the one on the other side, make the weather here uncertain. Sometimes, it gets trapped, like we are in a bowl. Other times, it skirts around us." He glanced at her. "Are you a fan of snow?"

She shrugged. "It's pretty. For a while. I don't like to drive in it, though."

"Same." Kenny turned left, down a small path. "I thought I'd take you to field two. It's a really special one."

"Why?"

"Well, about two years ago, just before opening weekend—before my sister knew Stuart—the field caught fire. All the trees for the season burned down."

"That's awful!" Merry said.

"Yeah. So, around here, the field numbers rotate, and the number indicates how old the trees are. So, right now, this is field two. These are the baby trees that were planted that year. Meaning the trees are two years old. A lot of folks paid for their tree in advance to plant them. Others adopted a tree, if you will. I've got one myself, and wanted to show you."

Merry laughed. "That sounds sweet. I'd love to see them. And your tree."

Kenny led her across the field, to a small tree all the way in the back. "For some reason, mine is the smallest, but I don't care. With enough love, she'll look special."

"Like in *Merry Christmas, Charlie Brown*?" Merry asked.

"Exactly."

"Where will you put it in your cabin when you cut it?" Merry asked.

"Oh, I won't keep it. I'll find a family who needs one and is having a hard time and donate it to them." Kenny shook out the picnic blanket near his tree and shrugged when he saw Merry looking at him. "What?"

"That's just...really kind of you," she told him. "I wasn't expecting to hear that."

He flushed. "It's nothing. It's just, you know...being human."

"The world needs more humans like you then," Merry told him, helping him unpack the picnic. "Imagine if we all thought more about helping others than doing stuff for ourselves. But then," she sighed, "imagination doesn't pay the bills."

"A roof over the head is important," Kenny agreed. "But so is doing things for others. And that's something I really like doing. Hungry? Chicken salad, crackers, bread, fresh fruit, vegetable soup in thermoses, and the cookies you surprised me with," Kenny told her. "Take your pick."

Merry reached for the soup, and poured some into a cup. She looked slightly nervous, and Kenny knew he felt that way too. They hardly knew each other, so what was he doing inviting her out for a picnic?

They ate for a few moments, and Kenny finally asked, "So, you know what I do. What about you, when you are not having a winter picnic at a tree farm with someone who is practically a stranger?"

Merry laughed, then her face clouded. "I own a marketing business," she said. "Though I don't know for how much longer. I might have to start filling out job applications. Which makes it all the more stupid that I even came out here, seeing as my financial situation isn't great, but I needed to get away for a few days. See if I could figure things out. Spark ideas."

"Business slow?" Kenny asked.

"Yes. It's been a hard year for a lot of people. I think I'll be okay if I can keep this one client. She's my biggest. Things will be tight, but I can keep going and build from there. However, she's not liked what I've pitched, and I've only got one more try to impress her." Merry pinched the bridge of her nose. "I just don't understand what she's asking for, I guess. Each time I send her something that I've come up with and think is what she's looking for, she turns it down."

"Is she hard to please?" Kenny asked, putting chicken salad on a cracker.

"Not really. At least, she wasn't before. But she's changing up her branding and wants to be different from everyone else."

"That could be helpful to attract new clients," Kenny agreed. "But what's she wanting?"

Merry scrunched her nose. He found it positively adorable. She pushed her blonde hair behind her shoulders, and said, "She's wanting playful and rejuvenating in a forest setting. I have no idea how to combine that, or really what it even means. It's all she's given me, and no ideas for a jumping off point.

"That's why I'm a little sour right now. I don't mean to be rude. Like yesterday, when you stopped by. I just had no idea I'd be surrounded by so much holly and jolly here, when I just wanted to wallow in my misery and figure this out."

"No biggie. You weren't rude." He gestured around. "Maybe this place isn't what you'd expected at first, but maybe you are here for a reason. I mean, this is almost a forest. We've got the cabins, trees. People come here all the time to rejuvenate. To play, too."

Merry only groaned.

Kenny wasn't sure what to say without making things worse, so he didn't answer, and instead peeled an orange and studied the scenery.

Perfectly shaped pines of many varieties. A few birds soaring overhead. Clean air, the scent of the freshly laid mulch, the squirrel that was watching them, rubbing its paws together... It was a setting that fed the imagination, restored the soul, and made you want to keep returning. This, right here, was part of the magic of the place.

Kenny wondered if this might be the key to making Merry smile. To save her job and give her some happiness. What if he could show her the small things all around them that added up to something amazing? Would that help?

He glanced at her sullen face. He doubted she'd be interested. Maybe he should just keep his thoughts to himself.

Kenny reached for the grapes and tossed a few toward the squirrel. He wasn't sure if they even ate them, but was rewarded with the little fellow snatching one up and nibbling on it.

"Aww! He's so cute," Merry cooed.

"And look there," Kenny said, pointing to a small bird hopping toward them. "I wonder if the little fellow got separated from his flock." He gently rolled a berry toward the bird, who took it in its small beak and flew away.

Kenny picked up another cracker. "At risk of sounding annoying, I'd say this has been one of those moments your travel agency is wanting. A picnic is ordinary. But in the winter? With animals coming up to you? Extraordinary. It's a chance to play, and explore. To do something different.

"I know for myself, sometimes when I'm having a bad day, just being here outside resets me. Makes me feel better. Just being in nature is rejuvenating. Ever heard of earthing? It's supposedly really beneficial health-wise. And nature in and of itself is playful. Especially for a kid full of imagination. A stick is never just a stick. It could be anything from a sword to a wizard's wand to a snake to a music leader's baton."

She grew a thoughtful look. "You could be right. I need to think on this some more. My best ideas come when they brew."

Kenny reached over for a cookie. "Same. So, if I talk too much, tell me to stop," he told her. "Meanwhile, I will keep pointing out things if I see them. Maybe something will spark an idea for you."

A gentle brush of Merry's fingers on his made him freeze. He looked up to see her smiling at him. "Thank you. Things might have started off a little rocky, but maybe being here is just what I needed."

CHAPTER 6

What was she thinking? Kenny was a stranger. And though she doubted he was anything more than a nice guy, Merry couldn't believe how she'd been acting. First, she was kind of rude. Then, she was all practically flirting?

Stress. That had to be it. There was no other excuse for her weird behavior. Zero.

Coming here had been a bad idea.

And a really good one.

She helped him pack up their picnic, and joined him strolling through Field 3, as he showed the difference a year could make.

When had Kenny explained how their picnic turned a normal, everyday thing into something special, and now there was more to something thank first glance, Merry almost glimpsed it. How those things could feel rejuvenating. Playful. Make a great ad. But just as quickly, it left. Maybe some more of those moments would happen—and she'd actually notice—so that she could start to write the ad copy. After all, this place was pretty similar to the one she was helping the agency book.

Merry shot a glance at Kenny. She'd never, ever felt so comfortable around a guy. Especially one she didn't even really know. What was going on?

"Something special," Kenny said.

"Huh?" Merry looked at him. Had he answered her question? She hadn't been talking out loud, had she?

"Look there," he said, pointing in the distance.

Merry let her eyes follow, and gasped in surprise at the two deer walking through the Christmas trees of Field 4. One had to have been a late born fawn, as it stayed close to the larger deer and looked at them shyly. "Wow! Does that happen often around here?"

"Not really," he answered. "That's why it's something special. Rejuvenating. At least, to me. Think about how you feel right now. Maybe feeling a little wonder? Curious what will happen next? Enjoying your time out here, just walking around and relaxing? Could be something is usable for your ad campaign."

"I guess you're right on all of that. I don't know if I'd have even noticed the deer unless you pointed them out," Merry admitted. "Or the fact that I am enjoying our time outdoors. I was just sort of being here. Not really thinking about it."

"That's how a lot of things are in life," Kenny said in a thoughtful tone. "We don't notice. I've missed out on my fair share of things. That's why when something does catch my eye, I make sure to tell whoever I'm with. It would be selfish to keep it to myself."

Merry gave him a sidelong glance. Kenny was so unlike anyone she'd ever met. The way he saw things, wasn't ashamed to admit his deeper thoughts, she had never been around such a thing. She found it made her reflect. Even want to change to be more like him.

"You know, this place is perfect. Last night, it was like a scene from a Christmas movie. Those lights, the music, people walking around…" She shook her head. "It was actually pretty amazing. I'd have regretted not venturing out."

"I'm glad you were here to enjoy it," Kenny told her. "Not everyone takes the time to notice what's going on around them. Small details are easy to overlook, but we sure put a lot of effort into them here. Even though I've been helping for a while, I'm still not used to that feeling of excitement and wonder that fills the air as it gets closer to Christmas here, and we start doing all these events. Actually, I hope I never do get used to it. Each time feels so special."

She was quiet, letting those words reply in her mind. Was that…was that maybe what had happened with her clients? Maybe she'd just gotten so comfortable with doing what she knew, she hadn't thought about innovative ways to make things special. Don't fix what's not broken, right? But did that mean she hadn't been listening when they told her they wanted something different? Especially her contacts at the travel agency, who had noticed their ad traffic dropping off.

That was also what clients wanted. They didn't want the same old with their vacation. Tammy was right. She did need different. Needed playful and rejuvenating, especially right now, when so many families were stressed. Apartment repairs aside, wasn't that why she was here? She was also stressed and tired and feeling stuck and hoping the trip would spark something for her. That was why people vacationed. To come back mentally refreshed.

In just a short time, Kenny had pointed out seemingly normal events, like an animal walking, but in a way where they felt special. How could she apply that to the travel agency? Especially the rejuvenating part?

The more she thought about it, the more she realized she was meant to be here. It was hard sometimes for Merry to relax. There was a pressure she put on herself to do well, to be successful so she didn't have to find herself searching the sofa for coins to help buy groceries like she remembered doing more than once as a child. It had made a lasting impression on her, and made Merry determined never to find herself in that situation again.

Being here, around someone who really had his eyes wide open to all around him made her want to live the same. Each moment filled with wonder and happiness. Peace. Was it possible, though?

Then, there was Kenny himself. She was really enjoying his company. When was the last time she'd thought that about someone, let alone a guy? She'd always been too busy with work. This easy conversation she had with Kenny, however, was something she wanted more of.

The cabins were in sight. They'd be splitting up soon, and she didn't want their time to end. Merry stopped suddenly, as sadness washed over her. It was foolish, wasn't it? To feel this way?

"You okay?" Kenny asked.

"Yeah. I just wanted to thank you one more time," Merry said, her hand reaching out with a mind of its own to touch his arm.

The tips of his ears pinked. "There's no need to," Kenny said, the pink spreading over his cheeks.

"I want to, though. Here, you've taken the time to show me around, made me lunch...it was really nice. You've also given me a lot to think about."

Kenny grew a thoughtful expression. "Come to the movie tonight."

That hadn't been what she expected to hear. She also hadn't expected her answer. "What's playing?"

"If you had the schedule," he teased, and she smacked at his arm. "*The Christmas Candle*," he told her, though his eyes were still laughing.

"Is that the one where the people in the town all hope they'll be given the candle that will make their wish come true? But it's faith that actually makes it happen for the whole town?"

"That's the one," he told her. "You've seen it?"

"I love that movie," Merry said. "Ever since I ran across it on TV one year, it's become a tradition for me. I'll be there."

"Tacos beforehand?" he asked. "My treat."

"You, sir, have sealed the deal," Merry said, feeling much lighter. It was nice knowing she'd see him again in a few hours.

They started walking again, and in too short of a time were at her cabin.

"I've got to work a while," Kenny told her. "One of the IT upgrades went wonky with our virus protection's newest update. But meet you by the food trucks around six?"

"Sounds good. Thank you again for the picnic. And showing me your little tree."

Kenny grinned and raised a hand in farewell, but when he got a few steps away and had a foot on his porch, he called, "Hey!"

"Yeah?" Merry asked as she looked over.

"What do you think about Christmas magic?"

"Huh? Like Santa?"

"Sure. Him too. Santa, the warm glow, the magic all around if you just look for it." He held his hands up like a pair of binoculars.

"I believe in hard work getting you where you need to go," Merry said, knitting her brows and wondering why he was asking such a strange question. "Maybe Christmas magic is real, but I've never had it for myself. So, I don't know."

"Where's the fun in that?" Kenny asked, dropping his pretend binoculars.

"Life isn't always fun," Merry said, crossing her arms. "There's a lot of stuff that honestly kind of stinks. Like what's happening to me right now. Sometimes people just don't want to be happy. They want to just...try and work things out on their own. Without relying on 'magic.'"

"Well, yeah, but life doesn't always have to feel that way. Maybe that's why you are having a hard time getting what your client wants. It's important to find joy. Even in small things. Like seeing those deer. That was fun. That was magic. But, that comes from a place of play. Of being relaxed enough to notice it. If you don't have that feeling in you, you might struggle to put it in the words your client wants."

She could see he was honestly trying to help, and shrugged. "Maybe you're right."

"I know I am. And I can tell you need more of that for inspiration, so I've decided I'm going to help you learn to look for it."

Merry raised her eyebrows. "Pretty sure of yourself, aren't you?"

"Yep. So how long are you here for?"

"Three more days."

"Three days." He nodded slowly. "I can do it."

She laughed. "Can you now?"

"Sure. Why, most Christmas movies are less than two hours, and it happens in those every single time."

The guy was crazy. But she actually didn't mind. He was also making her smile, and feel happier than she could ever recall being in her life.

"You know this isn't a holiday special, right?"

"Yep. But like you said, we've got the perfect setting for one. Maybe even better, since this stuff's real, not cinema magic. And who knows...by the end of those three days, you might just even fall in love with me."

Merry's jaw dropped, and then she rolled her eyes. She was still working out a reply to that when Kenny winked at her, and vanished into his cabin.

Give her a dose of Christmas spirit? Fix her business problem? And...fall in love with Kenny?

That seemed a tall order.

But...not an unappealing one.

Then, reality sank in as she stepped on her porch, and Merry groaned at the impossibleness of it all. Three days wasn't enough time to fix anything, let alone fall in love with a person.

Was it?

The smallest piece of her wished it could happen, but her practical side knew it was foolish to even hope for that.

Merry went inside, hung up her jacket, and sat down at her laptop and tried to come up with some ideas for Tammy's Travels.

Again, browsing competitors didn't come up with anything new. Neither did looking at ads for outdoor adventures or supplies. She tried various slogans and searched for stock images to convey what Tammy was looking for to put together a mockup.

Nothing looked right.

Their campaign was for a series of cabins in the middle of nowhere. There were few amenities. Merry rubbed at her eyes. What could she talk up? Rejuvenating... People could unplug. Get back to nature. It was forced relaxation since there wasn't much around, but playful? How the heck could people be playful? Play was for children, not adults.

"This is pointless," Merry groaned. "There's no way to make this special sounding. It's the woods. Not a theme park or a European vacation with sightseeing galore. And just relaxing isn't what she wanted. Rejuvenating is way different. It's energizing. Restorative."

Her fingers hovered over the keyboard. How could she make the ad come across as energizing? She thought back to her picnic with Kenny. "Surround yourself with nature's beauty? But everyone says that. That's not special enough. See the unexpected? Again, that's such a generic thing to say."

She closed the laptop and paced around, feeling her stress levels mounting. Eventually, she flicked on the TV and lost herself in a game show. Merry knew avoiding work wouldn't make things better, but neither would sitting there getting more upset.

A few episodes of *Family Feud* later, she studied herself in the full-length mirror in satisfaction. She hadn't brought much for her short getaway, but she was wearing the most festive thing she had, a red sweater with snowflakes under her thick coat and fuzzy hat and gloves. No one would see it, since it was too cold to take off her jacket, but part of her wanted to look nice for Kenny.

Merry didn't know why, but Kenny made her stomach do a little flip, and she was really looking forward to seeing him again. Tacos, her favorite Christmas movie, and Kenny. It was bound to be a good evening.

Maybe—just maybe—he'd already started to give her a bit of mood lifting.

Merry studied herself once more, this time wondering, did that mean the other two things might come true as well?

CHAPTER 7

Fall in love with him? Why did he say that? Oh, Kenny knew why. His brain had been thinking it. But why did his mouth betray him and spit it out before he had time to stop himself?

She hadn't looked upset, though. Merry's face had been one of surprise, and though she'd rolled her eyes, he'd seen a blush spreading across her cheeks. Maybe she hadn't minded. He wondered if she was feeling something for him, like he was for her. Things like that could happen quickly, couldn't they? Was he getting his desire to make her feel better mixed up with real attraction?

He knew he'd started out wanting to help her. Kenny still wanted that—more than anything. But he also wanted to spend more time with her. To hear her laugh, see that eye roll she did so often, how she crinkled her nose... She was intelligent, and interesting, and sarcastic. He loved the teasing side of her. There was a lot about Merry that he liked, and Kenny didn't want to stop being around her.

She didn't deserve to be so worried, to struggle. He hoped he'd be able to help her. To make her smile, not feel stressed over her job. It would be even better, though, even if it was a selfish thought, if in a few days they parted as really good friends.

Or more.

Kenny took a deep breath. Regardless of what might happen, he was going to push those thoughts away and get to work. He had to. The sooner he finished, the sooner he could see Merry again. How was it he was so interested in her so quickly? He felt the silly grin come over his face. The one that had only started when he met her. Now, it emerged each time he thought her name.

"I like her, Goldie," he told the fish, who seemed to nod her head at him. "I really, really like her. When I'm with Merry..." He didn't finish his thought. Saying it out loud, saying that she was giving him that thing that had felt missing was crazy. Wasn't it? He hardly knew her.

But he wanted that to change.

Goldie swam frantically and blew a few bubbles at him.

"You're right," Kenny agreed. "Work. Can't play until it's done."

Kenny opened his laptop and opened his program files. It was difficult staying focused when all he wanted to do was think about Merry and their day together, but just before five he finished, and shrugged his shoulders a few times to stretch them.

A quick shower later, Kenny headed outside to help Allison and Stuart.

As he approached the open area where they held the tree farm events, he saw the food trucks pulling up. Allison was plugging in the lights on the Christmas tree and the decorative white lights they had strung around, while Stuart was getting the popcorn machine going.

The scent of buttery goodness filled his nose and made Kenny's mouth water. He started to fill the white and red striped paper bags with popcorn and folded over the tops, then set them in neat rows for anyone who wanted to buy some.

"Need some help?"

Kenny looked over as Merry came up to him. "I've almost finished," he told her, "but I'm going to take you up on that tomorrow, if you are willing."

"Just ask," Merry told him with a smile.

"Good. No backsies," Kenny warned.

Merry laughed. "Uh-oh. I sense I walked into a trap."

He grinned. "You did. So, be ready tomorrow at 9 a.m. You might be a guest, but you offered. However, seeing as you are an extra special guest, I'll take you to a late lunch when we get done. With any luck, it won't be too late."

"Extra special, eh? I'll be ready," Merry said. Then she slid her arm through his, just as naturally as if she'd done it every day of her life. "Now, how about those tacos?"

There was a small line, which Kenny and Merry got into, but it didn't take long for them to get their orders, two tacos each and a large order of nacho chips covered in melty cheese and fresh salsa to share.

"I could get used to this," Merry said, as they ate their dinner. "It's kind of nice not cooking."

"I get spoiled this time of year," Kenny admitted. He hesitated, "Maybe you won't believe me, but I've also enjoyed having dinner with you the last two nights. Usually, I'm by myself. Allison and Stuart have me over sometimes, but there are days I feel a little like a third wheel so I don't always like to go."

"I understand," Merry told him. "The rare time I get together with friends, it's the same since they are all hooked up. And, even if we've just met, I'm glad we did. It's crazy how it feels like I've known you much longer than, what? Twenty-four hours?"

"Is that all it is?" Kenny asked, surprised. "I guess you're right."

"Kenny!" Allison called, waving her arms and then pointing at the sound system.

"That's my cue to get the movie started," Kenny laughed. "One sec."

"I'll throw away our trash and meet you over there," Merry said, grabbing it and heading toward the large bin set out.

Kenny jogged over to his sister. "Sorry if I interrupted the flirting," Allison said. "I tried, but it won't turn on and I could hear you in my head telling me not to break anything, so I stopped pushing buttons."

"We weren't flirting," Kenny said. Then he grinned. "Yet."

His sister laughed, and squeezed his arm as she walked past him and toward the popcorn.

Kenny got the movie started, then grabbed some popcorn bags and sodas, and went over to where Merry was just sitting down in a chair. He sat next to her, and offered the snacks.

As the movie continued, he couldn't help but sneak glances at her. He also wished they were sitting next to each other. They needed more benches here and fewer single seats. But then, he started to worry. What if she got the wrong idea? Thought he was trying to put the moves on her in a bad way? Yeah, they'd been maybe almost flirting a little. But facts were, she was a guest here. Maybe she didn't want serious. Just flirting.

If he'd been by himself, Kenny would have said a loud "gaaaah!" and scrubbed his fingers through his hair. Instead, he was forced to sit there and lose himself in the spiraling thoughts about if she thought he was a weirdo or not.

Luckily, Merry was lost in the movie, and soon he was too. Even if it was a little hard and he was on high alert each time she moved.

"I love that movie," Merry sighed almost two hours later as they walked back to the cabins. "A thought came to me as we watched. Maybe I'm also here, not just for a respite and work, but to be surrounded by all of this Christmas to help me recover a little of my own faith. Faith that things will work out. Faith in my own abilities. If I can just figure out what this client wants."

"I think you will," Kenny told her. "Might not be easy, might not happen right away, but I think it's going to."

"You're so...supportive," Merry said, stopping under the lamppost and studying him. "I'm a stranger. What do you care?" She quickly held up a hand. "I don't mean that rudely, I'm just curious. You're so genuine. So nice. I don't see that a lot. Could be because I don't get out a lot either, but I can't think of a time when I ever knew someone who was so caring toward others."

"I just..." Kenny wasn't sure if he should say it. So he shrugged. "I don't know."

"Yeah, you do," Merry told him. "Why?"

"I just want to see you smile," Kenny said softly. He brought his hand up, letting his fingers brush hers before he dropped his hand. "I don't know why. I'm not asking for anything in return. I just...I just want to help. If I can. That's the kind of person I am. I don't have a huge or tragic backstory. I grew up normal, I guess. Family of four. We love each other. Work hard. Try to be good people. I'm...I'm really pretty boring, and happy with the small things in life. That's it."

She was quiet for so long, Kenny started to get scared.

"Not everyone needs to have a backstory," she told him. "You can just be you, the way you are." Then, she pointed at the sky. "The stars are so pretty," Merry said, her head tipped upward. "So bright and clear." She met his eyes. "I just noticed them. And I wanted to make sure you did too."

Kenny smiled. "There's good and beauty and joy all around us," he agreed. "I'm looking at it right now." Even in this dim light, he could see Merry flushing. He cleared his throat, feeling suddenly shy, and pointed upward, trying to ease any awkwardness.

"We have really good open skies around here. It's fortunate, too, that it's clear most nights. Stars, constellations, galaxies, planets. Things far bigger than we are. It's kind of magical. Fuel for the imagination." He motioned a little to the right. "Those, right there. That's Orion's Belt. Even looks like one, doesn't it?"

"Yeah," Merry said. "I've never really looked at the night sky much. It's really pretty, and you are right. There's so much there. I just wish I had your gift to see more than what meets the eye."

"Here," Kenny said. He took her hand and closed his eyes, squeezing them tightly.

"What are you doing?" Merry asked, her voice curious.

"Giving you some of that ability," he said, releasing her hand.

Merry's eyes opened widely, but she didn't say anything. They stood there for a long time, saying nothing, even though the space between them was filled with a tension Kenny had never felt before. He wished he knew what it meant. It wasn't bad, but it was heavy. And he felt nervous about doing anything to make it go away, or change in another direction.

Merry finally let out a soft sigh. "I should go. Goodnight. See you in the morning."

"See you," Kenny told her, and jammed his hands into his coat pockets.

He watched as she went to her cabin, then went up the porch to his and let himself in. Sleep didn't come easily. Each time he closed his eyes, he saw glimpses of Merry's face. Her too-brief smiles. The sadness that sometimes flickered in her eyes. He wished so much that he could do something about it.

Three days. Could he do it? Make her happier? Help with her job problem? He was sure going to try. He also had a lot to do around the tree farm for opening weekend, so was looking forward to both her helping him tomorrow, and the chance to help her.

And, if something more grew between them? He'd be just fine with that. But if it didn't, it wasn't meant to be, and he wasn't going to push her. He wanted Merry's happiness, whether it was with or without him.

When the sun rose, Kenny was ready. Promptly at nine, he knocked on her door.

"I'm ready," Merry greeted him. "Where to?"

"First, the fields. Stuart's been up since five getting some of the trees cut. You get to help me haul them from the field to the stand and set them up."

"That's not what I expected to hear," Merry said, "but okay. Let's go."

"You can back out," Kenny said. "No hard feelings."

"Nope! Let's go. I get to show off my muscles. That doesn't happen often."

He laughed, and led her over to Stuart's old truck. A large flatbed trailer had been hitched to it. As Kenny opened the passenger door for Merry, she asked, "Do you really put your guests to work?"

"We don't normally," Kenny said, "only when a few ask. Then we find some small thing for them. But I wonder if we should do it more often. They have working ranches...why not a working tree farm?"

"Not a bad idea," she agreed, and closed the door behind herself. Kenny jumped in, and drove out to the first field. Several small trees lay, already cut.

"We drag them on the trailer like this," Kenny explained. "And once it's full, take them back. There are tree stands there waiting for us to pop these in. Believe it or not, we'll sell most of them this weekend."

"People don't want to cut their own?" Merry asked, pulling one of the trees toward the truck.

"A lot do, but we also get local businesses that want trees, but aren't particular on which they get. Sometimes people have already cut one, but then think of someone they'd like to give a tree to, and don't want to go hunting again. Having a bunch already cut makes their choosing much easier."

"I see." Merry stepped back and brushed some hairs that had come loose from her braid out of her face. "That makes sense. There are so many trees here! Thousands! They smell wonderful."

"It's a kind of magic." Kenny nodded. "So's the good feeling of seeing them all lined up in the ground. There's something special in it. I like to imagine the faces of people when they choose their tree, and the joy it's going to bring them over the coming few weeks." He hesitated. "It's also really nice, you being here. I appreciate your help, but I'm really enjoying your company."

Kenny didn't know what she'd say about that, and Merry didn't actually say anything, but he was rewarded with one of her beautiful smiles before they climbed back into the truck and headed for the next field of trees. On the short drive, Kenny tried not to feel nervous, but his palms were sweating, even with the chill in the air.

How was it she made him feel this way? Nervous and happy and so many other things he couldn't explain. Did she feel it too? She had to, right?

"So, you get some trees from different fields, I guess based on size?" Merry asked as they got out and started to load the trailer again.

"That's right. Some people want a small tree. Others love the biggest they can get. What kind do you set up at your place?" Kenny asked.

Merry stretched her arms apart. "I guess it's about three feet? It's prelit. All the work is done for me."

"Easy peasy," Kenny agreed. "I used to do that too. But now, I'm crazy over the real thing."

"But what do you do with it, when Christmas is over?" Merry asked. "Just throw it out? That kind of seems wasteful."

"Here, we mulch them if anyone brings them back. Some people put the branches in their gardens for wintering. Others burn the wood in their fireplaces. Since two or three are planted for each one cut, and this is done commercially, it isn't like just going into the woods and taking out a tree."

"Makes sense," Merry said. "Maybe I'll buy one of these small ones before I go. It would be a good souvenir."

"When Christmas is over, maybe you can bring it back for mulching," Kenny said. "Then I can see you again."

Her cheeks turned pink, and he was sure it wasn't from the exertion of pulling on another tree. Merry gave him a long look, and just as Kenny started to worry she'd slap him or something, she smiled and his heart started to pound.

"Maybe I will."

CHAPTER 8

"I had no idea how much work went into running this place," Merry said, stopping to drink from the bottle of water that Kenny had given her. "Whew, this is exhausting. I hadn't expected that."

"It really is, and I feel like I'm taking advantage of you," Kenny said uneasily, looking over at her. "You don't have to help. In fact, I insist. Want to sit down? Or head back to your cabin?"

"No way! I like helping," Merry said.

"Are you sure?" Kenny asked, doubt all over his face.

She laughed. "Are you worried you'll get a bad review from me?"

"We've had a few," he said with a grin. "A favorite is, 'Came all this way and forgot to buy a tree we were having so much fun.'"

"Wow! Really?" Merry asked, her eyes wide. "They one-starred for that?"

"Wasn't a one star," Kenny said and winked. "We are sitting at a perfect five."

"Fact check," Merry teased, whipping out her phone. Once she pulled up the tree farm on Google, her jaw dropped. "You are right. You guys are nearing a thousand reviews! Wow! Perfect rating. And I don't plan to leave anything less myself. Now, let's get back to work." She took another sip of her water, then added, "This place doesn't run itself!"

"For sure, and Allison and Stuart work hard to make the tree farm enjoyable for everyone," Kenny said.

"So do you," Merry said. She screwed the cap back on the bottle. "Don't forget about yourself."

"When you enjoy what you do, it's not work," Kenny told her. "And I enjoy most every minute. Ready for our last job before we grab a bite?"

Merry nodded. "What is it?"

"Allison had this idea of snowflake lights and an archway and making it like a magical entrance for people to walk through after they park." Kenny frowned. "That's all she said, and I don't know quite what to do, but I have a garden arch and the lights. I guess we start there and see what happens."

"Let's do it," Merry said. "It'll look great!"

She and Kenny put the archway at the start of the path that led to the opening where Kenny told her local vendors would be set up. Carefully, they wrapped the snowflake-shaped lights around the wide archway, putting most of them at the top as though they were falling from the sky.

Kenny had two more boxes of white fairy lights, and they used those to wrap around the sides of the archway. "These all have a slow twinkle feature," he said. "I think that's what we will use."

"I can't wait to see it," Merry said. "Will you have them on tonight?"

"Sure will!" Kenny said. "I think it's going to look really good."

Merry adjusted one of the snowflakes near the top of the arch. "I agree. Anything else?"

Kenny pulled a checklist out of his pocket. "We got the trees from the field and put them in stands. We put all the tables out, and added the garlands on the fronts. We got the ribbon-making supplies out. We decorated the smaller trees for the tables. We decorated the Candy Cane Tree with the candy canes donated by the grocery store—all six hundred of them. Well, except for that one that broke and we shared. We did the arch."

"Phew! We did a lot," Merry said. "Anything else on there?"

"Nope. Just a visit to the diner now. I'm pretty hungry."

"Me too," Merry said, and followed Kenny over to his vehicle, a gray SUV.

He held the door for her, and she climbed in, sinking into the leather seat. "This is really nice," she told him when he got in and shut the door.

"I love it," he told her. "Bought it from a turned-in lease. Couldn't believe my luck!" He started the engine and eased down the gravel road. "It's about a ten-minute drive. Not too far."

"This town looks a lot nicer now that I can sit and look at it and not worry about finding my way," Merry said. "You wouldn't believe the trouble I had getting here."

"Oh no!" he said worriedly. "We have all these signs! Where did you run into trouble? I'll let Stuart know."

"No, no, the signs were great," Merry answered. "I mean beforehand." She told him about her wayward GPS, and then the flat. At first he laughed along with her, and then he groaned. "Oh, geez. You really have had it rough the last few days," he said. "I hope that being here has brought a little bit of relaxation."

"Between all the hard work I'm doing and didn't expect?" Merry teased.

"Hey, work makes you sleep better at night," he answered.

"Then you must sleep really well," Merry said. "I've never been around someone who works so hard."

"I can't answer that," Kenny said, glancing at her before his eyes returned to the road.

The air in the car felt different suddenly. Her chest tightened, and she saw Kenny's shoulders were tense too.

"Why not?" Merry asked.

"Oh, uh, just one of those things people say," Kenny answered. "Anyway, this time of year, there's always so much to do, sometimes I worry I'll forget something." He tapped his head. "Got the ol' to-do list up there. Keeps me up at night as I go through it."

"Somehow," Merry said, her voice slightly sarcastic, "I'm not buying that. Is that the real reason?"

He hesitated, then shrugged. "Oh yeah, haven't you ever had a lot on your mind that's kept you awake?"

"I have," Merry said, "but my to-do lists aren't one of them. Won't you tell me?" When he stayed silent, she said, "Never mind. Sorry. I don't mean to pry."

He glanced at her again, and softly said, "You aren't prying, and I don't mind. It's just that you might not like my answer. And, I work at the tree farm you're at. So, maybe I shouldn't say it. I don't want you to think I'm a creep or something."

"Now I really want to know," Merry said. "What makes you think I won't like your answer?"

Kenny took a deep breath. "Because you might not want to hear that I've not been able to sleep since I met you. That every time I close my eyes I see you."

Merry felt her pulse speed up. She knew Kenny was looking at her, and she met his eyes, briefly, before he had to look at the road again. "I've never had anyone tell me that," she said softly.

"I hope it was okay. I mean, I know we just met and all." He pulled into a parking lot and stopped the car. "Here we are," he said. "And, I hope I didn't just weird you out."

Merry shook her head. "Nope. But, it made me wonder if you were working on that plan of yours."

"Which plan?" he asked.

"To make me fall in love with you," she answered.

"I wasn't," Kenny admitted, but then he gave that grin she'd really grown to like. "But does that mean it's working?"

She laughed, and leaned over, surprising both herself and him as she kissed his cheek before letting herself out of the car. "Maybe."

Kenny jogged ahead of her to get the diner door, and the moment they walked inside, the scent of French fries and pot roast and chocolate cake hitting her nose, Merry felt ravenous.

"Get yourselves a seat," the hostess called out.

"That's Wilma," Kenny told her. "Been here since they opened almost fifty years ago."

"Boy, she must love her job," Merry said. "I can't imagine working at the same place for fifty years." She slid into the chair and grabbed one of the slightly sticky laminated menus against the napkin holder. "What's good?"

"Everything." Kenny studied his menu. "I like the BLT, but the burgers are great too. So are the fries."

"Know what you want?" Wilma asked, coming over with a small notepad and pen.

Kenny looked at her, and Merry nodded. "Iced tea," she said, "and the BLT with fries."

"I'd like the same," Kenny said. "But with a Coke, and what's the pie of the day?"

"Caramel apple," Wilma said. "You'll love it."

"And two slices of that for us," Kenny said. "Thanks, Wilma."

"Back shortly, hon," she said.

Wilma left, and then brought their drinks before either she or Kenny had time to say anything.

"Thanks for helping me today," Kenny told her as he took a straw from the holder placed on the table.

"I didn't mind," Merry told him. "But I won't lie, I was sort of hoping that something would spark a few marketing ideas. No luck. Maybe tonight, when everything is lit up."

"It will happen," Kenny said. "When you force things, it doesn't always work."

"You're right on that," Merry said. She sighed. "I've got to get her something tomorrow. I just wish I could understand a little better what she's looking for. You seem to."

He was quiet for a moment, then said, "Not necessarily, I'm just guessing. Playfulness and rejuvenation are all around us. I don't say that because I'm trying to make you feel bad, but it's those small moments that everyone always misses. It just happens. Maybe some people don't even realize it. I wonder if your travel agency place is trying to show that to others. That if they book with her, they'll get the stuff they didn't even know they needed."

"Like what?" Merry asked. "Can you give me an example? I don't think I'm following."

Their food arrived just then, and Kenny grabbed the ketchup and squirted it into the shape of a rainbow, complete with a little pot of gold. "Someone might call that playing," he said with a wink, "but I call it art."

She laughed. "I don't know if I can use ketchup art in my ad copy, but I admit, that's playful. You look like you've done that a lot."

Kenny grinned. "Oh yeah! Like I said, we've been coming here since we were kids. I'd be bored out of my mind sometimes, either waiting for my food or waiting for others to hurry up and finish. Hence the ketchup art I'd do, with my last few fries."

"What did you do while waiting for your food?" Merry asked.

He pointed to the wall. "See those red stripes along the wall?"

"Yeah?"

"When I was a kid and we would come here, I always wanted to sit along the wall, so I could race my little toy cars along the stripe. It wasn't a painted stripe, it was a road and I was the driver."

"That's so cute," Merry said.

"And this table here," Kenny said, "is my favorite because if you look just so, you can see the large clock tower that chimes every half hour. I used to pretend it was the signal for something."

"Like what?" she asked.

"Anything. A warning, like in the old days. A gong summoning a magical dragon. A song played for us here in town, to make us happy. Doesn't matter. It was all those things and more. If I forgot my car, I'd use the salt and pepper shakers, and whatever else I could find to do pretend battles with or play some other sort of game I made up."

Merry smiled, imagining a young Kenny entertaining himself. "You really are the epitome of play," she said, giving a small laugh. "And...weird as it sounds, I feel rejuvenated around you. So now that I see you are what I'm looking for," she teased, "I just have to figure out how to get you on paper."

He winked, smacking the table. "There you go! You can do this, Merry. You can give them what they are looking for. I know you can."

Lunch was over too soon, even though they both lingered over the pie. Kenny told story after story, and Merry let herself be swept away. He had quite an imagination. If only there was a way to bottle the things she felt when she was with him. She'd be sure to give Tammy just what she wanted for the ad.

As they drove back, they listened to Christmas songs playing on the radio and she had to admit, she'd never felt quite so happy.

"I'll be Home for Christmas" played, and then everything came crashing back. Merry swallowed hard. Home. She'd be leaving soon. Her time here was almost up. What was going to happen then? She kept feeling like something was growing between herself and Kenny, and Merry really didn't want to let it stop. Not if it could be something good.

Though she hadn't gone out on a lot of dates or hung around a lot of guys, she'd done enough to know that until now, she'd never really connected with one the way that she was connecting with him. What did that mean? And what was she supposed to do?

"We'll figure it out," Kenny said softly.

"How did you know what I was thinking?" Merry asked.

"Maybe I don't," he told her honestly. "But it seemed like something I needed to say."

They pulled into the gravel road and got out of the SUV. Kenny walked her to her cabin and stopped, his eyes searching her face. "Thank you for everything you did today."

Merry shook her head. "I think you did more for me than I did for you. Anyway, I had fun."

His hand reached for hers, and he gently squeezed it. "Hey, I have to run some errands tomorrow. I know the last thing you probably want to do is run around place to place, and I know you have your job stuff you need to do, and you paid to enjoy a relaxing weekend..." He stopped. "Sorry. I'm rambling. I do that when I get nervous."

"Don't be nervous," Merry said, squeezing his hand. "What is it you were starting to say?"

"Well, tomorrow, do you...you want to join me? It's okay to say no," he added in a rush. "But it's Christmassy, at least I think so, and I thought maybe you'd enjoy it."

"I'd love to."

He grinned, and Merry felt her stomach do that little flip again. She liked his smiles. At this moment, she would have said anything to keep seeing it pointed at her.

"Okay. See you soon." Kenny walked backward to his cabin, then waved at her, the grin on his face matched by the one on hers. They both went inside at the same time.

However, reality crashed down around her again when she spotted her laptop on the kitchen table.

With a sigh, Merry sat in front of her laptop, hoping she could deliver. She tried to rekindle those feelings Kenny gave her. That energy, how everything felt like it was a game or an adventure waiting to happen.

But three hours later, she had nothing and put her head into her hands, holding back a sob. This was it. She was almost out of time. That silly glimmer of hope she'd had about keeping her business alive...that's all it was. Silly.

And so was what she felt for Kenny. It had to be. There was just something about this place. That's all. The vacation charm. Didn't loads of women fall in love in books while on vacation? This was no different, just a true-to-life thing. He was so incredible, and she was...she was boring and uninteresting, and soon to be without the client that she needed to stay afloat. He really wouldn't want her then. A woman who couldn't even manage to take care of herself?

Merry pushed her laptop away, and laid her head on her forearms, letting her frustrations and hurt dampen the table.

CHAPTER 9

"Thanks for doing this," Allison said. "Stuart's really disappointed he can't, since he does it every year, and you know how much he enjoys it. But since Carl's in the hospital, he needed to go visit and stay for a while."

"You know I got this, sis," Kenny said. "I just hope Carl starts to feel better."

Carl was Stuart's longtime employee. He'd been out in one of the fields trimming trees, and fell from a ladder, breaking his left arm and leg, and injuring his head. It was lucky Stuart had been nearby, and the old man hadn't been left hurt until he was found.

"Me too," Allison said. "Hopefully he's back home in a few days. I hear his niece is going to move in and help him recover."

"That would be good," Kenny said. He took the company credit card and slid it into his wallet. "And don't you worry. I asked Merry if she'd like to join me. Should be a fun outing."

"Kenny, I'm not sure that's a good idea. Does she know what you are doing?" Allison asked hesitantly. "Remember, it's got to stay secret. We don't know her."

"You don't, but I do," Kenny said confidently. "Don't worry. She won't tell anyone. I'm sure of it."

"All right, I trust you," Allison said. "I'm swinging by the hospital real quick too. I'll be back in a while."

"See you," Kenny said, walking away toward the cabins.

He headed over to Cabin #2, and knocked. The door opened almost immediately.

"I'm ready," Merry said. "Where are we going?"

"It's a secret," Kenny said. "The whole day is. So, when we get there, you can't tell anyone. Ever."

Merry stopped mid-step. "Sounds serious."

"It is. But not in a bad way. It's just...well, Stuart does this every year. And his dad did it and his dad, as long as Pressman's has been around. He can't this year, and since it's kind of time sensitive, I get to do the legwork. But it's a secret," Kenny said, leading her over to his SUV. "And you have to promise to keep quiet."

"I will," Merry said. "As long as it's not a criminal activity."

"Far from it," Kenny said. He slid into his seat and said, "It's as far from it as one can get."

"Curious," Merry said. "I can't wait to find out what it is!"

"Can you be my GPS?" Kenny asked.

"I'll be better than that," Merry laughed.

Kenny drove, following the directions Allison had given him on a printed sheet of paper. Merry read them, and they found their way to the large house situated on a corner. A tall metal fence surrounded it, and children's play equipment could be seen behind another, smaller fenced area.

"What is this place?" Merry asked.

Kenny hesitated. "It's a shelter. For women and their kids. And I need you to remember not to tell anyone about anything we do today. You promised."

Her eyes wide, Merry nodded, and followed him as Kenny knocked on the front door.

A woman opened it and smiled at him. "Kenny! Come inside. Your sister said you were on the way. Who is your friend?"

"This is Merry," Kenny said. "She's playing elf to my Santa today."

"Wonderful," the woman said. She nodded at Merry. "I'm Martha. We have quite a list for you this year. It's a few more people than last time. Are you sure..." She stopped, concern growing on her face.

"Great, let me have it!" Kenny said, rubbing his hands together and ignoring the question that had been started. It didn't matter how many were on the list. Pressman's would provide for each.

Martha nodded and handed Kenny a large envelope. "Before you leave, do you want to see the tree the children decorated?"

"Yes!" Kenny said, following the woman who ran the shelter down a small hallway. She led them to the living room, where the tree, a six-foot spruce, rested against a wall, decorated in candy canes and shiny plastic balls and paper snowflakes.

"It's beautiful," Merry said.

"Sure is," Kenny agreed. He pulled out his phone and snapped a few pictures. "I'm going to text Stuart these photos. He always puts a lot of time into picking the perfect tree for you guys, and seeing it is always such a highlight for him."

Martha smiled at him. "Thank him again for me, won't you? And tell Carl I said to heal quickly."

"Will do."

Kenny followed Martha back to the front door and left with Merry. When they got to the car, he held the door for her, and then climbed inside, opening the envelope.

"What's that?" Merry asked, looking at the papers he pulled out.

"This," Kenny told her, "is tradition. It's the wish lists of the children who live there, looks to be twelve of them this year, and their mothers. The moms we give gift cards to, for a ladies' clothing store. But the children we buy gifts for. Clothes, toys, books..."

"That's incredible," Merry told him, taking one of the lists. "How do you manage to afford that?"

"Stuart always sets aside some money throughout the year. I asked him once what would happen if there wasn't enough, and he told me it would happen somehow. It always seems to. But that's why we keep trying to grow the farm, so we can do more and help more people. He does something similar for the nursing home too. We might expand the cabins from eight to ten next year, and the year after get to a dozen. They stay full, and the more visitors we have, the more that can be set aside to the giving fund."

Merry was quiet. She finally spoke as he pulled onto the street. "So I take it this is an anonymous donation? That's why you don't want anyone to know? Or me to say anything?"

"Yeah," he told her. "I mean, Martha knows, and the owner of the clothing store, and the toy store. But no one else does. At least, I don't think so."

"I'm grateful you trusted me," Merry said. "I can't wait to help you with this."

"It's a lot of fun," Kenny agreed. "I'm really glad I get to share this with you. Toys first! It's my favorite."

He pulled into the parking lot of the toy store. "You're going to love this place. At least, I hope you will. Then it won't seem too weird how much I do."

She laughed, but the sound died on her lips as they walked inside and awe took over. Walton's Toys was an old-fashioned toy store. It was filled to the brim with everything any child—or child at heart—would want.

Rocking horses and plush toys, dolls, action figures, toy cars, blocks, puzzles, and balls, tea party sets, and games filled every shelf and display. It was impossible to walk inside and not leave with something. Merry felt pulled in a dozen directions at once, and like she never wanted to leave.

"Kenny!" Mr. Walton said eagerly as he rubbed his hands together. "Got the lists? This is my favorite time of year."

"I do," Kenny said. He looked at Merry. "You want the girls, and I'll take the boys?"

"Sure," she agreed. "How do we do this? Is there a usual plan?"

"Yes. My sister is strict. She wants every child to have a book, a plush, a soft blanket, and three toys. You can go by the lists for some suggestions," Kenny told her, handing her five lists.

"Got it." Merry started to walk away.

"If you go child by child, I'll wrap up the gifts. Set each child and their list here on the counter when you're done," Mr. Walton said. "I'll give back the lists when you are done so you can have their clothing sizes."

Kenny thanked him, and browsed the store. He could see Merry doing the same, running her fingers over dolls and teddy bears.

Two hours later, Kenny paid for the toys, and left the store. Mr. Walton would deliver them, so no one knew who they came from.

"Clothes next," Kenny said. "We actually can just stay parked here. It's just a few buildings away. You up for a short walk?"

"Sure!" Merry said. "I love looking in the decorated shop windows."

"Me too," Kenny said. "Everyone's got fun displays this time of year, and it feels really festive."

They walked along the sidewalk, and Kenny wished he were brave enough to hold Merry's hand. So, when her fingers bumped against his, he couldn't help but grin. It was close enough.

"Here we are," Kenny said, holding open the door he'd stopped in front of.

"Welcome," Mrs. Miles said as they walked inside.

"Got the toys." Kenny grinned, leaning on her counter. "Now the hard part!"

She laughed. "If you need help, let me know. Otherwise, I'll be here wrapping the outfits."

They repeated the process again. A warm jacket and a pair of shoes and three outfits for each child.

As Kenny went to pull out the credit card, Mrs. Miles held up a hand. "One moment," she said. "I need to punch in the employee discount."

"You don't have to do that," Kenny told her.

"Oh yes, I do," Mrs. Miles said, and her voice wobbled. "It was Stuart's father who took care that my little Gracie and I had a Christmas the two years we were at the shelter back when I was a young mother with nowhere to go. I'll never forget how it felt, knowing my girl had what she needed because of that man. The Pressmans are good people. You too, young man."

"Yes, they are," Kenny agreed, his eyes feeling moist. He glanced over at Merry, who was wiping her eyes on her sleeve.

"I'll send them over, dears. That way no one knows," Mrs. Miles said. "I'm overjoyed to be playing a part in this. Now, you run along and leave this part to me."

Kenny nodded, took the receipt, and left, holding Merry's hand. "Thank you," he called as they walked outside.

They got back into his car, neither speaking on the walk. Kenny started to put the key in, when Merry's hand rested on his. He looked at her. Her beautiful eyes were shining with unshed tears.

"Thank you for letting me come along," she said. "This was unexpected, but so incredibly wonderful to be a part of."

"I can't think of a better person to share this with," Kenny told her, meaning every word.

They drove back to the tree farm, and Kenny felt content. He was enjoying his time with Merry. He knew she would be leaving soon, but before she did, he planned to ask her out. It wasn't difficult at all to imagine spending more time with her, and he no longer had that fear she wasn't at least a little bit interested in him.

Just as they pulled up to the cabins, Merry's phone trilled. She fumbled in her purse for it, grimaced as she saw the number. "I have to take this. It's the travel agency."

He nodded, and waved to her as she headed toward her cabin, talking to the caller. The look on her face was one of concern, and Kenny hoped nothing was wrong. Maybe he shouldn't have invited her. She needed the time to work.

They'd had such a good day together, and Merry had been smiling for much of it. So, maybe she had been okay with it. Kenny sighed. His wish he'd placed on the tree had come true. He just hoped hers would too.

CHAPTER 10

"Not a problem. You'll have those tonight," Merry assured Tammy, with far more confidence than she felt.

The call disconnected, and Merry dropped her phone back into her purse. Nothing. She had nothing. No ideas at all. Not a single one.

She closed her eyes for a long moment. But instead of the travel agency's needs coming to mind, she saw the shelter. Martha. The tree decorated so lovingly. The lists given to Kenny. Piles and piles of toys in the most magical toy store she'd ever been in. Mrs. Miles at the clothing store who had been emotional as she discounted the items and shared her story.

Merry had felt that way too. And she could hear Kenny saying that somehow, it always worked out. But, how? Things hadn't for her. Not her whole life, and this was just another example. She felt selfish thinking such a thing. After all, she could get another job somewhere. It might not be for herself, in the thing she'd built, but that didn't mean her life was over.

That she was a failure because she had let herself dream.

Merry found herself momentarily lost in the memories of her own childhood Christmases. They'd struggled, and sometimes there weren't but the necessities in life. Sometimes, there hadn't even been those. Memories of her childhood's bleak Christmas mornings came to mind. Though it was silly, the longing for the toys she'd never had rose up.

Swallowing hard, she thought how excited the kids here were going to be on Christmas. And, in some small way, she was helping.

She drew in a deep breath. It was time to stop feeling sorry for herself. Ground up, she'd built her business. But then a little voice whispered, she hadn't been able to keep it, had she? And all because she didn't have the imagination she needed to be creative enough to deliver to her clients.

Imagination... Merry's eyes narrowed. She blamed her grandmother who'd raised her for that. The woman had been very strict. At any hint of pretending, Merry was scolded. Why pretend to cook dinner when you could be efficient with your time and do the real thing? Why play with dolls when you'd be an adult soon enough with children to care for? Read a fiction book? It didn't expand the mind! A waste of time! Daydreams—any kind of dreams at all—were pointless. Only hard work counted.

While Merry knew she'd been blessed not to be without a roof over her head, or food and clothing, she realized now just how bleak things had been, and how her current situation could be attributed to that. Maybe that had been her grandmother's excuse because she hadn't had the money to buy those things, but Merry honestly couldn't remember any fun as a child. That was what made it so hard.

She looked around the room. What could she see to make things feel extraordinary? Playful?

There was a potted plant with freckles on it. If she connected the dots, it might make...no. That was stupid. The clouds through the window. They were shaped like...clouds. Merry dropped her head into her hands. "I can't do this. I can't. I don't know how Kenny does it. I'm not playful, and this...this isn't rejuvenating. It's stressful."

A loud knock startled her, and she jumped up, heading for the door. When she opened it, Kenny was standing there.

"Hey," Merry said.

"Hey," he answered. Kenny shuffled his feet a little. "I got the vibe you needed a friend."

Wordlessly, she opened the door and he walked in.

"Got some sodas," Kenny said, pulling two cans from his pocket and offering them to her. "Want one?"

Merry took the lemon-lime drink. "Thank you."

"If I'm in the way, just tell me to go. I know you have to work," Kenny told her.

"They want the ads tonight, to show at a meeting tomorrow," Merry said, cracking open the can of soda. "I don't have anything. This is it. Judgment day, and I've failed."

"No, you haven't," Kenny told her firmly. He took her drink from her, then set both sodas aside and put his hands on her arms, giving her a little shake. "You've got this! Maybe I can help."

"I appreciate the offer," Merry sighed. "But I think this is it. I'm out of ideas. It's useless."

"No, you aren't," Kenny said. He dropped his hands. "I believe in you."

"You hardly know me," Merry said. "Yet, from the moment we started talking, you wanted to help me. Why?"

"I'm...I'm a fixer," Kenny said uncertainly.

"That's it? That's the only reason why?" Merry knew she was getting louder. She was also starting to get angry. Her chest was tight and her breathing came faster.

"No, there's a lot more," Kenny said, his own eyes flashing.

"What is it then?" Merry asked. "If you have something to say, say it."

He turned away from her, and went to the window. The air felt charged, but not in a good way. Merry could see Kenny's jaw clenching, and she bowed her head. "I'm sorry," she whispered. "I shouldn't have taken my stress out on you."

Kenny said something, but she didn't catch it. "What? I couldn't hear."

He turned to her. "I said, I don't understand why. But the moment I saw you drive up here, I felt this weird pull. And I wanted to get to know you. Help you. Be with you. Make you smile." He stepped closer to her. "Merry, I don't know why, but I really like you. And so, yeah, I want to help you. Not because I want anything in return, but because I just want you happy."

The space between them seemed to hold its breath. Merry stepped closer to Kenny, and before she knew it, her head was against his chest, and his arms were around her. She breathed in deeply, and he smelled a little like pine. That made sense, didn't it, him living here?

"Even if you can't keep this client, things aren't over for you. They aren't ruined." Kenny's voice was firm, yet comforting. "You love what you do. I can tell. So don't give up, Merry. Because I won't."

Merry sighed, and pulled back enough to see him. "When I was a kid, I wasn't allowed to play pretend," she told him. "These last few days, and then today being around all those toys, it's made me realize, I think that's why I can't see things the way you do.

Playfully. Those things don't refresh or relax me, because I don't know how to do it. It just makes me stressed out."

He was quiet for a moment, then picked up their drinks and walked to the sofa. Merry joined him, taking her soda.

"If you could have had imaginative toys, what did you want?" he asked her.

Merry didn't have to think hard. She knew right away. "An Easy Bake Oven," she told him. "And a Barbie. And one of those clear candy canes, with candies inside. I know it's just candy, and not really a toy, but I always thought they were so neat."

"Ohh my sister loved those things as a kid," he said. "She cooked all kinds of things. Even if the oven took forever to make anything. She tried to make us cookies once. After two hours of waiting, I got bored. They were ready that night just before bed. Finally. I thought they'd never bake. It was tiny too. Like, one bite's worth."

Merry laughed. "I hear that about them. I imagined that I would have made a feast—or so I thought—for my Barbie and me. The candies would have been magical ones, and brought her to life."

She watched as a smile came over Kenny's face. "That sounds really cool," he told her.

"It would have been fun," she told him, then took a sip of her drink.

"Did you see what you did there?" he asked. When she shook her head, he said, "You said, 'I imagined,' and then you told me what." He tapped his head. "It's in there, waiting for you, once you relax and let it out. Listen, the client is a client. You can get another if you need to. Facts are, not every person is right for every job, and not every client right for every company. Doesn't matter which it is in this situation. But one bad experience doesn't mean the end of the world.

"So what if you can't give her what she wants for her ads? Maybe she really is wanting something that doesn't exist for what she's trying to sell. Maybe the things you were suggesting were what she needed, but she's too stubborn to care. At the end of the day, you're doing your best, and that's all you can do. The final decision is hers. And don't let that define your worth.

"She's got to do what she thinks is best for her company, and you've got to do what's best for yours. Maybe that means you look for clients who align with you, not the other way around."

Merry realized she was nodding along slowly. "You know, you're right," she told him. "I've always given my best, and that's what I'll do again. I can't make them like it. And if they don't, someone else might. The ideas I have she didn't want, I can still use."

"That's right," he told her. "So don't give up. Give it one more try. If it happens, it happens. If it doesn't, you're going to get something better."

Merry smiled. "I think you're right. I feel a lot better too. Thank you."

"I—" Kenny stopped as his phone rang. He dug through his pocket. "Hey, sis. What? Ohhhh. Yeah, I'll do that. Give me five; I'll be right over."

He stood, and apologized, "Sorry, I've got to go get the cider order for tonight. Stuart got a flat, and Allison has a work meeting."

"Totally fine. I've got an ad campaign to create," Merry said, standing as well.

"Before I go, one more thing for you," Kenny said. He reached into his jacket pocket, and pulled out a small glass jar. "Here."

"What's this?" Merry asked, looking it over. She could see it had previously held olives. At least, that's what the lid said.

"I know it looks empty, but it's not," Kenny told her. "You know this place is filled with amazing moments. So, I bottled some up for you. It's an old jar, but it's what's inside that counts. So, if you need it, take the lid off and breathe in deep."

Merry would have laughed had he not looked so earnest. It was also kind of sweet. "Thank you," she told him, standing on her tiptoes and brushing her lips against his cheek.

Kenny's cheeks flushed, and he grinned. "See you tonight."

She nodded, and watched him through the window as he left. Once he was out of sight, she turned back to the table and her laptop, clutching the empty olive jar to her chest.

Merry sat and started to put the jar down, when she instead unscrewed the lid and cracked it, just a bit, and breathed in deeply. She didn't smell anything different, well, maybe a hint of brine, but it didn't matter. If Kenny said it was there, she was going to believe him. She was going to have faith, just like in the movie.

Now. Time to get to work.

CHAPTER 11

"Thank you for getting the cider," Allison said as she handed a copy of the order to Kenny. "This claim is requiring a little more work than any of us at the insurance company could have predicted."

"Happy to do it. I love cider as much as anyone else," Kenny told her. "Maybe more. So we can't go without it. I'll save a jug back for Carl. I know he always gets one."

"Good idea. You are so thoughtful. I appreciate you getting so much done around here the last few days," Allison said. "Stuart and Carl said to thank you. You worked so hard. I can't believe you got it all done."

"Merry helped me," Kenny told her.

His sister laughed. "You're honestly making our guest work? I knew she went with you for the toys, but you had her helping the other times? She wasn't just chatting with you?"

"Well...yeah." Kenny shrugged.

"Do I sense anything between you two?" Allison asked.

"I don't know. I'd like there to be, but I'm not sure yet. It feels like there might be, but it's kinda soon to know, I guess. I don't know. This isn't something I have much experience in."

"She's cute. You'd look good together. Mom would think so too," Allison said.

Kenny flushed. Before he could say anything, his sister added, "It's nice to see you so focused on someone. I don't know if you ever have been."

"Part of it's because I'm trying to help her," Kenny said.

"How?"

"She's trying to save her business."

"And working around the tree farm is helping her do that?" His sister arched a brow.

"She's got a huge marketing campaign to write, and I'm, hopefully, giving her ideas for what the owner of the travel agency wants."

"Uh-huh." Allison smiled. "Whatever. I think it's sweet. And typical Kenny. Always got to fix things."

"Why shouldn't I? Isn't the whole point of being a good human to help others?" Kenny crossed his arms.

"Just teasing, little brother. Yes, it is. But are you sure you're doing this to help her because you want to? Not because you feel like you have to? I just don't want to see you hurt, if it turns out that she's not really interested in anything beyond her time here." His sister looked at him worriedly.

"I won't be," Kenny said. "I'm doing this because I want to. It makes me happy to help others, okay?" He scowled. "Now, let me get going before the cider place closes and everyone is disappointed. You know that's a top seller. If I don't make it there in time, I'm telling everyone it's your fault. You want to make Carl cry? He's already hurt enough."

"Right. Sorry," Allison said, shooing him away. "Go."

Kenny left, and cranked up his radio as he drove off. He still felt a little upset about what his sister had said. He'd told Merry a few times he liked her. But, just now, he realized she'd never said the same.

It didn't matter. He just wanted to help her. And if Merry didn't like him in the way he cared for her, there wasn't a thing he could do about it.

Two hours later, the back of his SUV was filled with crates of freshly pressed cider. As Kenny drove through town and stopped at the traffic light, something in the toy store window caught his eye. When the light turned green, he pulled into the parking lot and got out, making sure to lock the car so nothing happened to the cider.

As he pushed the door in, Mr. Walton looked up from where he was reading the paper. "Well, hello there, Kenny. You forget something?"

"No, just thought of something else I wanted," Kenny said.

"Take your time, look around. Whatever you see I can gift wrap." Mr. Walton went back to the newspaper, and Kenny took a slow lap around the store. A short time later, he asked, "Okay if I take this from the window display?"

Mr. Walton looked up. "Go ahead. That's the last one."

"Thanks. I'll take this, and be right back." Kenny walked down an aisle and stared at all the choices before him. No wonder kids took so long in the store. It was mind-boggling how difficult it was to pick.

Finally, he grabbed a box off the shelf, and then stopped at the Christmas stocking stuffer display near the register.

"That it for you?" Mr. Walton asked.

"Yes. And you said you could gift wrap it?" Kenny asked.

"Sure can. What kind of paper do you want?"

Kenny looked over the choices, and picked one with small Christmas trees on it. A few moments later, he was leaving the toy store with his purchases.

CHAPTER 12

Merry paced around the cabin, running over to her laptop each time she heard the sound of an email come in. An hour before, she'd sent over her ideas to Tammy. She was anxious to know if they'd be well received.

Since the ad was going to be an outdoor family excursion, Merry tried to capture every detail of what she'd done and felt and seen and experienced the last few days.

Her second night, while they were watching the movie, she'd noticed a few children playing off to the side. One boy had been looking around through binoculars. One little girl was sketching leaves and acorns she'd collected. Others were also involved in various activities, and they were all electronic-free, but very filled with imagination. At the time, she hadn't paid too much attention to them, instead focusing on the movie and her time with Kenny, but as she looked back, she saw the children were really enjoying the nature around them. They were playing, and had so much energy. It was obvious that had come from being there on the tree farm.

Merry added those ideas to her mock up, including the dad hunting for rocks and the mom remembering her childhood trips while she snapped photos. She'd made other suggestions as well, including taglines and graphic suggestions, and clicked Send.

She refused to second guess herself. Either Tammy liked them or she didn't. Merry had come to the conclusion that play and rejuvenation wasn't just seeing or experiencing things in a new way, like Kenny had tried to show her. It was also about letting yourself simply enjoy your surroundings, and being present in them. That's where the magic was. That's where the ordinary moments became special.

And, maybe, that's also what Kenny had been trying to tell her. She wasn't sure. Imagination was still so hard to grasp for her. But Merry felt really proud of that thought forming.

She knew without a doubt that the tree farm had been instrumental in helping her see that. Kenny had been as well. Merry wondered if she'd ever get to see him again. If she gave him her number, would he call? He'd hinted about her coming back to mulch the tree she bought...and he'd told her that he liked her.

But she also knew that didn't mean he'd go out of his way to find her once she left. And since she'd been too shy to tell him how she felt, maybe—

The email chime sounded, and Merry nearly threw herself into the chair. This was it. She nervously clicked open Tammy's email. It was short and to the point.

Merry, I love them. Send over the contract for another two years. I've got a friend in toys. I'm going to send him your contact info. I bet you'd be perfect.

She'd loved them.

And a possible new client too.

A surge of relief washed over Merry. Suddenly, she felt very drained. Evidently, this had been more exhausting than she'd realized.

Merry let herself take a moment to recover, then sat up. She wanted to tell Kenny. Thank him for all of his help. Tonight, she'd buy him dinner at the food trucks. She grabbed her jacket, opened the door, and burst out, then stumbled backward as she collided into something strong, firm, and unmovable.

A hand grabbed at her, saving her from landing on her backside.

"You okay?" Kenny asked.

Merry looked up to see him juggling a few wrapped packages. "Yes. I'm sorry! I was coming to look for you."

"You found me!" he laughed. "Good news?"

"Yes! Want to come in?" she asked.

He followed her inside, and set his packages down on her kitchen table. "What are those?" Merry asked.

"Good news first," he told her.

Merry couldn't stop the smile that nearly split her face in half. "The travel agency liked my ideas! They are signing another two-year contract."

"That's great," Kenny told her, his face lighting up. "I'm really excited for you."

"Me too. I'm just so relieved," Merry said. "So, if you can, dinner tonight? It's on me."

"Sounds good to me," Kenny told her. "And it seems like it's the perfect time for these, since we're celebrating." He pushed the wrapped packages toward her.

"What are these?" Merry asked.

"An early Christmas gift," Kenny told her. "And, when you leave, something I hope you'll remember me by."

"But—"

"No buts! Open!"

Laughing, though she felt a little awkward, Merry unwrapped the largest first, carefully pulling the paper with the small trees on it away. She gasped as she saw what was under the wrapping paper. "An Easy Bake Oven!"

"That's right," Kenny said. "I mean, maybe you use it, maybe it sits on a shelf, and yeah, it came a little later than you wanted...but now you've got one."

Merry set it down and then wrapped her arms around him tightly and squeezed. "Thank you. It's perfect," she said, her words slightly muffled through his sweater.

"Keep going," Kenny told her, squeezing her gently, then releasing her. "There are two more."

She nodded, and eagerly opened the next one. Then, Merry started to sniffle. Inside was a Barbie, dressed in a snowflake dress.

"I thought the snowflakes might remind you of here, when we hung them," Kenny said quietly.

"They do. They will," Merry said, a catch in her voice. She looked up at him. "I'm going to miss you when I leave."

"I'll miss you too," Kenny said. "I was hoping we could maybe trade numbers?"

"I'd like that," Merry told him.

"One more," Kenny said, scooching the last one toward her.

When Merry picked it up, it made a curious rattle. As she peeled back the paper, she laughed. "A clear candy cane with candies inside!" Merry set it down on the table. "You shouldn't have. And I don't have anything for you."

"I'm not asking for anything. The world isn't always give and take. Sometimes it can just be give," Kenny told her. He looked deeply into her eyes, and Merry felt her heart speeding up. "I want you to always have the things you want. Even if they are small."

"What if I want something that would be tricky to wrap?" Merry asked, studying his face.

"Then I'd like to make that happen," Kenny said.

Merry smiled, and wrapped her arms around him again, nuzzling her face against the soft sweater and breathing in deeply. She loved how he smelled like the trees here. "I'd like that too," she told him.

"So...want to give me an idea of what it is?" Kenny asked, holding her close to him.

"You. I'd like you."

"Now, that I can make happen."

She held her breath and looked upward, as Kenny dipped his head and brushed his lips against hers. Warmth filled Merry, and she snuggled into his arms, her head back against his chest. Nothing had ever felt so right or so perfect.

CHAPTER 13

Kenny helped Merry up into the trailer full of hay. They settled on a spot, then squished closer as others joined them under the starry sky.

"Hang on!" Stuart called from the tractor, then pulled away slowly. They were moving at a pace Kenny could have outrun, but that just meant it would take longer to arrive back where the cocoa and cider were and he got to spend more time with Merry.

He and Merry had gone out to choose her tree from the field. It sat at their feet now, a cute little two footer.

"Isn't the sky so pretty?" Merry asked.

"Almost as pretty as you are," Kenny said, delighted by her laugh.

When the tractor pulled up, he helped Merry down. "Just a sec," he told her, then started to unload the trees for the guests. Merry waited for him, and when he'd finished, they walked toward the warm cider.

Allison handed them two cups, and Kenny led Merry toward the food trucks. "What do you want? Mac and cheese? Tacos? BBQ?"

"Tonight's a special night," Merry said. "It's also my last. So...how about I get us all three?"

"A woman after my own heart." Kenny winked.

They ordered two tacos, a plate of BBQ fries, and a bowl of mac and cheese topped with extra cheese to split.

As they sat down and ate, they were quiet. Kenny looked at the time. It was going by too fast. "Only a few more hours until you leave," he said quietly. "I'm really glad you came and we got to know each other."

"I am too. You opened my eyes to a whole new world. Saved my job. Saved me." Merry studied him. "I owe you a lot."

"You owe me nothing," Kenny said firmly. "Remember. It's not give and take."

She was quiet a moment, then said, "You were so right, that this place was what I needed."

"I'm often right." Kenny grinned. "Much to my sister's dismay. Only Goldie doesn't argue with me."

She laughed, as was his intent. "I still need to meet Goldie. I wish I didn't have to leave. I'd like to get to know you better. Spend more time with you." Merry lowered her head. "I'm going to miss you," she said softly. She reached into her jacket pocket, and pulled out a piece of paper. "Here."

"What's this?" Kenny asked, taking it.

"If you open it, you'll find out," she teased him.

Kenny unfolded the paper. On it was a large red heart along with what looked like a phone number and email address.

"I meant what I said earlier. So, this is my heart," Merry explained. "I'd like to give it to you for real. If you want it. And that's my number and email. So we can chat, whenever."

Kenny's chest tightened as he reached for her hands. "I want that. More than anything. I know this was soon. But..."

"When you know, you know," Merry finished.

Just then, it started to snow. Small flakes quickly turned into fat ones. All around them, people laughed and shouted or squealed with delight. Adults and children stood, catching the flakes with tongues or fingers.

The soft white lights around them made the snow twinkle. Merry stood too, her face lifted toward the night sky as she moved in a slow circle with her arms wide. "It's so beautiful!"

Kenny moved closer, and when she stopped spinning put his arms around her. "Could become a blizzard," he told her. "Then it wouldn't be safe at all to leave tomorrow."

"But isn't someone else going to need the cabin?" Merry asked.

"Nope. Allison told me they had to cancel. No charge if you want to stay a few more days," Kenny told her, trying not to sound too hopeful. "I know people. I can make it happen. I can also take off work. It can be just us. Whatever you want to do. No work."

"A blizzard, huh?" Merry said, and held out a hand to catch one of the icy flakes. "And no work for you?"

"That's right. A blizzard." Kenny nodded, as though he knew what he was talking about, even though he knew the weather tomorrow called for unseasonably warm temperatures.

Snowflakes decorated Merry's hat, and nose, and eyelashes, and she looked up at him, giving him the thing he'd longed most to see. Her smile. His heart squeezed, and he knew he'd never forget this moment. It would be imprinted in his mind forever.

"Well, then I guess I'd better stay," Merry said, leaning into him. "Just you, me, and the snowflakes all around."

WANT MORE?

Read Allison and Stuart's story (and how Kenny saved the day!) in No Insurance for a Miracle
When Pressman's Christmas Tree Farm goes up in flames only weeks before Christmas, Stuart seeks help from his insurance agent. However, he wasn't expecting her to be a female version of Scrooge. Allison doesn't like Christmas and could care less about the upset man in front of her, handsome or not. Fresh trees are wasteful, bad for the environment, and what kind of grownup makes his living in selling Christmas cheer?

Other than giving the minimum payout, she doesn't have any personal interest in the case. To be honest, she hates Christmas. It's filled with nothing but bad memories.

Stuart is praying for a miracle. Allison just wants to put the whole season behind her. Then she discovers some of the reasons Stuart is so desperate to save his farm and make it a success.

Will Allison let herself get caught up in the magic of the season? Can a Christmas miracle really happen not just for him, but her too?

https://www.amazon.com/gp/product/B0CBTDJ5 GR

***

Curious about the other book mention? A Sleigh Ride for Charlotte

Sometimes the simple choice isn't easy.

Charlotte Harrison dreams of being part of the winter festival, where romance fills the air and new starts are made. Penniless after her family was swindled, she's always stayed home, unwilling to be looked at with pity. But this year Charlotte is desperate and willing to do whatever it takes to be there when she hears the most eligible man in town has his eye on her.

New to town, Dr. Justin Davis is in dire need of someone to assist him at his practice. When Charlotte is suggested, it seems like an opportunity for them both. At first, he simply wants to help her financial situation. But against his better judgment, he falls in love with her. Worst of all, the man she desires is someone he can't stand, and he might have just sent her straight into his arms.

Through a series of surprising events, Charlotte learns that not everyone is as they seem, and when she goes to give her heart away, she's faced with uncertainty. Who is she going to choose? The man she's been longing for? Or the man who truly loves her?

https://www.amazon.com/Sleigh-Ride-Charlotte-ebook/dp/B0CW1JWNNF

NOTE FROM AUTHOR

Thank you for taking the time to read *Snowflakes All Around.*

Could I ask for one small favor? Reviews like yours on Amazon mean so much to me and help others to find my books! Even just a single line means a lot!

Also...

Want a FREE book?

Stop by my website to get your no strings attached **FREE book**. It's my gift to you, as a thank you for reading this one.

www.sarahlambbooks.com

ABOUT THE AUTHOR

Sarah writes captivating characters and clean romance that's anything BUT boring! From heartbreaking moments to heartwarming tales, get swept away in either historical or small town romance that pulls you in until the last page.

Nestled in the Blue Ridge Mountains of Virginia where she's married to her Texan husband, you'll find Sarah creating her next book, homeschooling her two boys, or volunteering in her community.

Want more of Sarah's books? Find them all on Amazon!

https://www.amazon.com/stores/Sarah-Lamb/author/B098H3SGLK